Internal Memo: Co...
From: Dr. Guy Giro...
To: E.R. personnel

After reviewing patient reports from Thursday night, I would like to commend all of you for your hard work and professional expertise during what's now being billed as the Storm of the Century. Although I was unable to be here because of the storm, I have received nothing but praise and gratitude from the fire and police departments, as well as civilians, on the performance of Courage Bay Hospital's emergency room staff.

As many of you know by now, one of the patients admitted was my stepdaughter. Heather was given excellent care by the admitting staff, and I know that all of you who dealt with her, especially Dr. Rachel Browne, worked tirelessly on her behalf.

I also want to thank you for the concern you've shown me during this time. Because of the extra work due to the storm, as well as my personal situation, schedules will be less flexible and some of you will be asked to cover extra shifts. I appreciate your willingness to do this, and suggest that anyone who finds the commitment onerous should address their concerns directly to me.

As I have always known, our E.R. staff is one of the best in the country.

CODE RED

JO LEIGH

NIGHTWATCH

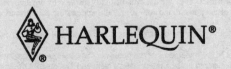

HARLEQUIN®

TORONTO • NEW YORK • LONDON
AMSTERDAM • PARIS • SYDNEY • HAMBURG
STOCKHOLM • ATHENS • TOKYO • MILAN • MADRID
PRAGUE • WARSAW • BUDAPEST • AUCKLAND

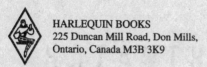

HARLEQUIN BOOKS
225 Duncan Mill Road, Don Mills,
Ontario, Canada M3B 3K9

ISBN 0-373-15332-5

NIGHTWATCH

Copyright © 2004 by Harlequin Books S.A.

Jo Leigh is acknowledged as the author of this work

www.eHarlequin.com

Printed in U.S.A.

Dear Reader,

Welcome to the next adventure in the Code Red series.
I had a fascinating time with this book, diving deep into
the world of medicine and emergency rooms, which was
a blast! I talked to a lot of nurses, particularly the terrific
Tammy Strickland and Myrna Temte, who made sure I
wouldn't make a fool of myself. Then I got to work with
the other authors of the series, which made it too fun.
As for the romance, well, let's just say I was able to use
some of my own experience to make it all come alive.

Let me know what you think. I promise I'll get back to you!
http://www.joleigh.com

Best,

Jo

To Marsha. Thank you. Again.

CHAPTER ONE

THE MOMENT Dr. Rachel Browne stepped outside to the emergency bay, the wind and rain slapped her in the face. So hard, in fact, that she had to hold on to the door to keep her balance.

The ambulance had slogged through what was already being called the storm of the century by the media, taking almost fifty minutes for what should have been an eight-minute ride.

The EMTs pushed open the doors, and John Wilkins, one of the E.R. orderlies, ran up to help them pull out the gurney.

Rachel, inadequately dressed in her lab coat, waited just under the overhang, but even so, she was soaked by the time the patient got to her.

"Julie Bell," the paramedic closest to her shouted over the wind. "Found on her bathroom floor, presumed overdose. No suicide note, but a lot of empty bottles."

"Any narcotics?" Rachel asked as they hurried into Courage Bay Hospital.

"Not that we saw. She's lethargic, but arousable. BP's 110 over 65, pulse 80."

"Julie," Rachel said, trying to get a response. "Can you hear me?" She looked back at the paramedic. "How long?"

"Maybe an hour. A friend found her."

"Where is she?"

"A tree fell on her car—she couldn't get out."

Rachel turned back to her patient as they hit trauma two. "Julie, what did you take? What kind of drugs?"

"I picked up everything I could find on the floor," the paramedic said, handing the bag to John.

They moved her parallel to the E.R. bed, and Amy Sherwood, a first-year resident, and two nurses, Katya and Karen, spaced themselves to make the transfer.

"On three," Rachel instructed, and they lifted the young woman with practiced ease.

"We're out of here," the paramedic said. "It's a nightmare out there. I wouldn't be surprised to see Noah building the ark. Man, I've never seen anything like this."

Rachel nodded at the man, then turned back to her patient, who'd roused enough to try to sit up.

"Leave me alone," she said, her voice slurred and wet.

"Lie back, Julie. We're going to help you, but you need to help us. What kind of drugs did you take?"

"Nothing, let me go."

"CBC, chem panel, blood and urine tox screen," Rachel instructed Katya. "We're going to have to pump her stomach."

"I'll get a tube."

"Wait." Rachel raised her hand, stopping Katya. "What were the drugs?"

The nurse opened the bag the EMTs had left. "Diazepam, doxepin, amaryl, aspirin."

"Pulse ox is 96 on 2 liters. I'll run an EKG. It could be tricyclics."

"She's tachy at 120," Katya said.

Rachel bent over the girl. "Julie!"

"Sats down to 81."

"Okay," Amy said, "She's lost her gag reflex."

"Let's intubate." Rachel grabbed the tube and got it into position. "Push flumazenil, .2 mil." Just as she prepared to open the girl's mouth, Julie stirred, then sat up.

Rachel took a quick step back. "All right, then. That's good."

"What's going on?" Julie asked.

"Do you remember taking pills?"

"What?"

"Let's give her charcoal and get her something dry to wear, please. Amy, you take it from here." Rachel walked out of the trauma room, shedding her gown and gloves. It had been like this for almost ten hours now, only most of the patients had storm-related injuries. Blunt trauma, electrical shock, traffic accidents. Which wouldn't have been so bad if any of the damn medical staff were here.

She wasn't completely alone, but every doctor who had made it in had been pushed to the limits of endurance, literally running from patient to patient, and there was no end in sight.

"Incoming!" John Wilkins yelled as he stepped on the floor pad, activating the automatic door. A man in a uniform stumbled in carrying a drenched woman. She had passed out or was dead.

Rachel ran to the woman while Wilkins and two others got a gurney. "What happened?"

"She's pregnant," the man said, gasping for air. "She was in my cab and she started having seizures. She passed out about ten minutes ago. Before that, she said her head was killing her."

"Thank you," Rachel said, shoving the Good Samaritan aside. She'd immediately recognized the symptoms of preeclampsia.

Katya came running to help, and as they pushed the gurney, Rachel told her to get a CBC and do a chemstrip. "And get me an OB."

Thunder rumbled as they headed toward Trauma 3. The girl, name unknown, roused when they transferred her from the gurney. She looked very young, pasty and full-term. She opened her eyes briefly, then shut them tightly as if the lights were terribly painful.

Rachel moved to the bedside. "What's your name?"

The girl mumbled incoherently.

"That's okay. We're going to take care of you and your baby."

The ghost of a smile flickered briefly as the nurses, Lydia and Katya, got busy with her vitals.

"BP is 250 over 70, and oh—"

The girl went into a seizure, her body spasming as if she'd been hit by a live wire.

"Give her 5 milligrams Dilantin. And get respiratory down here. We have a precipitous delivery, people, so let's get the kit and the crash cart. Where is my OB?"

"There is no OB."

Rachel looked up to see her resident, Amy Sherwood, at the door, donning her gown. "They have no one to send. We have to do it here."

Rachel held back her curse. She could do this. She would do this.

Lydia, one of the best E.R. nurses Rachel had ever worked with, moved in close, preparing the woman for a C-section.

"Amy, work on her BP," Rachel said, as she picked up the scalpel. "Where's anesthesia?"

"Right here, Dr. Browne."

Rachel didn't even look up. She knew it was Dr. Reid, and he could handle the next step. She pushed a stray hair from her young patient's face. "You're going to be okay, honey. What's your name?"

"Heather. Heather Corrigan." Even those few words seemed an appalling effort for her and Rachel had to lean close to hear.

"Hello, Heather. I'm Dr. Browne."

Heather's lips curled in a faint smile and she half nodded before her teeth clamped again as another labor pain hit.

Rachel swabbed her forehead while Lydia prepped her belly. "Who's your doctor, Heather? Do you have an OB? An obstetrician?"

Heather rolled her head back and forth in a negative response that obviously cost her. "Haven't seen a—a doctor. I need to see…" Her already weak voice faded into nothingness as another wave of pain swept her body.

Katya raced into the cubicle carrying the FHD–100—a portable fetal monitor that ran on batteries. "I've got another orderly coming down," she said. Then Reid covered Heather's mouth with the mask.

"All right then," Rachel said, putting on rubber gloves. "Let's be on top of this, people. Everything's going to be fine."

ONLY, EVERYTHING WASN'T fine.

Rachel peeled off her paper scrubs and threw them furiously into the trash. She never got used to losing a patient. At least the baby would live, although his heartbeat was irregular and his jaundice was advanced. If only Heather had seen an obstetrician when she'd first gotten pregnant. Or even come to the hospital a few hours earlier.

Desperate for some coffee, Rachel headed toward the call room, but John Wilkins flagged her down from the other side of the hall. She stopped wearily and waited for him to reach her.

"Sorry, Doc. EMTs are bringing in a guy who had a roof cave in on him in the storm. They'll be here in five."

"Oh, Lord. Okay, when he gets here, can you get him cleaned up and into X ray and then come get me?"

"Sure, Doctor." He paused midturn. "You okay?"

She looked at her watch. Almost 3:00 a.m. She'd been on duty for nearly seventeen hours. "I have to be, John. There's nobody else."

He nodded sympathetically. "I'll take care of it." He turned and hustled down the hall.

This time, Rachel made it to the coffee machine. She practically guzzled the first cup and was halfway through the second when John returned.

"He's in X ray, Doctor. Whoa. They need you, stat."

"That bad, huh?"

The orderly nodded.

Rachel slugged back the remainder of the coffee. "Well, let's hit it."

As she and John reached the X-ray room, the technician was just wrapping up. Rachel nodded and smiled at her, then approached the body lying on the gurney.

She noted approvingly that John had installed a saline drip and oxygen feed on the patient. She understood the orderly's reaction. The face of the man on the gurney was in worse shape than many of the traffic accidents she'd seen—a palette of cuts, bruises and swelling distorting the features beyond recognition. "What's his name?"

"Bruce Nepom."

The man's salt-and-pepper hair was matted with blood and he showed no signs of consciousness.

"Let's get him in one," Rachel said. As they walked, she pulled a small flashlight from her pocket and gently pried the man's eyelids open, one at a time. She flashed the light across his eyes, but the pupils were blown—dilated and unresponsive to the light. "Bruce— Mr. Nepom. Can you hear me?" As expected, there was no reaction.

Rachel examined the man's mouth. Three of his front teeth were broken, but he hadn't bitten his tongue.

Once they were in the exam room, she pulled the sheet back to expose a well-developed chest with a smattering of graying hair, and a massive bruise along the ribs.

She noted John had already put in a catheter, and that most of the man's injuries were upper body. She ran a finger along a tattoo on the man's left shoulder—two dragons entwined around a Celtic cross. The tattoo had once been colorful, but the tints had faded and darkened.

"According to the EMTs, the whole roof fell on him," John repeated.

She pulled on a fresh pair of rubber gloves. "Let's see what we can do to help Mr. Nepom."

RACHEL HANDED HER NOTES to the admitting nurse in the E.R. "Hang on to these for me, will you, Karen?"

"Sure, Doctor." She gave Rachel a quick once-over. "You look beat. About time you went home."

Rachel glanced at the half-filled seats in admitting. Aside from the two serious operations, she and Amy had treated dozens of broken limbs, stitched up God knows how many cuts, and even treated a man whose foot had been caught under a falling tree by poking through his toenail with a red-hot paper clip to relieve the pressure. She smiled at that one. "That's my plan, Karen. I'm hoping to sleep uninterrupted for a good twenty-four hours."

"Good night, Doctor. Or rather, good morning."

"See you later." Rachel headed out the double doors to the parking lot, still worried about Nepom. The surgery had been a success, but that didn't mean the patient would live. Even if he did, his head wounds were so severe she doubted he'd regain anything like normal consciousness.

Although the sun was actually rising behind her, she felt as if she were coming out of a movie matinee. It was as though she'd forgotten what natural sunlight was like. Standing on the steps a moment, she took a deep breath. Clean air, sunlight.

Great time to go to bed.

With leaden feet and a killer backache, she made her way across the debris-strewn lot to her car. It would take her ten minutes to get home. Twelve minutes to be in bed.

DR. GUY GIROUX CLIMBED over a fallen palm tree then up the rise at the edge of his property. From there he could see the road and, thankfully, the city maintenance crew hard at work disentangling the trees and cars that had prevented him from getting to the hospital the previous night.

The last he'd heard from the E.R., before his cell had gone dead, was that they were critically understaffed. As head of the E.R., he should have been there. Thank God Rachel had made it in, but with this kind of storm, the injured would be more than any one doctor could handle.

They should have been better prepared, given the run of bad weather they'd been having. It was only a couple of months ago that the last severe storm had come through, causing major mudslides that had washed away houses. Now this.

He headed back to his house, which mercifully had been spared the worst of last night's storm. His neighbor's ground floor had been flooded, and Mrs. Allen had come to him for help, but all he'd managed to do was get her and her three annoying Pomeranians into the warmth of his spare room.

It was the only thing that had gone right. Without television reception or phone service, he'd relied on his radio for any word of relief, but it hadn't come till about an hour ago.

The storm was the worst recorded in the history of Courage Bay, California, and he knew firsthand how far back that history went. His great-great-great-grandfather, Pierre Giroux, had been the captain of an American twenty-one-gun sloop of war, the *Ranger,* which had blown off course during the U.S.–Mexican War and been shipwrecked in Courage Bay. Perhaps in a storm like this.

Guy heard the dogs yapping before he crossed his threshold. He liked dogs and ordinarily wouldn't have minded their incessant barking, but not today when he was suffering from lack of sleep and a rare feeling of helplessness.

"Dr. Guy?"

He inhaled deeply and let the air out slowly, trying to ease the headache that had been building steadily from four this morning. "Yes, Mrs. Allen?"

"The babies are hungry. Do you think it's possible to get into my house and get some food for them?"

"No, I don't believe it is. But I have some ground beef in the freezer." He closed the door behind him and headed for the kitchen, avoiding the small woman still dressed in her housecoat and curlers.

"They'd like that very much," she said.

As he got the beef out, he turned to her. "I'm going to have to leave. The road is open, and I'm needed at the hospital. The power's back on, and I'm sure they'll have the phone service turned on shortly and you can call your sister."

Mrs. Allen nodded. She was eighty if she was a day, and her sister was only a few years younger.

"Then you call your insurance agent. He'll help you with the house."

The woman sat down at the dining room table, and the dogs, none of them puppies, swirled around her legs, panting heavily. "Thank you for last night. I don't know what we would have done without you."

"It was my pleasure." He put the beef in the microwave, hit defrost, then excused himself with a reassuring smile to get ready for work.

His shower, although too brief, revived him somewhat, and the three aspirin would help even more. By the time he'd dressed and returned to the kitchen, the dogs were gobbling up their breakfast, eating out of his cereal bowls. Mrs. Allen stood watching them, and he was glad that she had them. Everyone needed someone to care for.

She looked up at him with a coy grin. "Have I told you about my great-niece, Lilly?"

He nodded. "You have."

"She's a very beautiful girl, Doctor. And she can cook like a dream."

He grabbed his coat from the back of his dining-room chair and slipped it on. "I'm sure she can, but I'm already married—to my work."

"Oh, I'm sure—"

"If you don't believe me," he said, "you can ask my ex-wife. Turns out I don't share well with others. So save your niece the grief."

Mrs. Allen sighed. "It's such a shame. You're so very handsome, and especially nice."

He touched the older woman on the shoulder. "Thank

you. You have my phone number if you need anything, right?"

She nodded.

"Please let me know when you reach your sister. If I'm not available, you can tell my secretary, Connie."

Mrs. Allen went back to the pleasure of watching her "babies" as Guy headed toward the garage. He pressed the door opener as he stepped inside. The garage was neat as an operating room, which was the only way he'd have it. Inside, his baby, a 1958 Corvette, sat shiny and polished as the day she was born. But he wouldn't take her out today. Not with the roads so torn up. Instead he climbed into his Range Rover and prepared for a slow twenty miles to the Courage Bay E.R.

When he arrived at the hospital, his headache returned full force. He went to his office first, but the usual piles of reports were missing. As was Connie. He played back the messages on his private line, and after two calls from a pharmaceutical house in Boston asking him to speak at a symposium next spring, Connie's voice came on, letting him know that she'd been stranded and would get in as soon as the streets were cleared.

Guy sighed as he went to make coffee. His office wasn't large but it had its pluses, the main one being the private call room. He busied himself with coffee grounds while he thought about the missing reports.

He'd have to give the staff the benefit of the doubt. Considering the conditions last night, reports weren't the top priority. Saving lives was.

Which meant that he would take his coffee to go.

He'd do rounds, assess the situation in the E.R. But first, more aspirin.

The scent of his Kona coffee made him feel better as he went back to his desk. He kept meaning to replace the old thing, with its battered sides and stiff top drawer, but whenever he had any time off, he made his way to the boat.

Just thinking of the *Caduceus* relaxed him more than anything else in the world. His '44 sloop was everything a man could want in a boat, and his only regret was that he had so little time to sail her.

Thank God she'd been in dry dock during the storm. She was getting a new mast, aluminum. He was to have taken her out next week, but with this damn storm…

He'd call. After rounds.

Coffee cup in hand, Guy walked toward the admitting desk, all thoughts of sailing firmly stowed away. Before he reached his destination he was stopped twice, once by Karen, the admitting nurse, then by Mike Trailer, the head of maintenance, both of whom had tales of woe. Karen was concerned that the computers had been down for two hours during the night, and Mike told him about some window blowouts on the third floor. He listened patiently, although he was sure the information had already been given to Callie Baker, the chief of staff. He was more concerned with what was happening now in his domain.

Surprisingly, there were only four people in the admitting area, none of whom presented serious problems. Two of the E.R. bays were occupied, one with a woman who had broken her left hip when she fell on a toppled tree, and the other with a heart-attack victim, who was now stabilized.

He went back to admitting, and when Karen gave him the charts, he flipped quickly through the various cuts, bruises and breaks. He stopped when he got to Bruce Nepom. After reading the chart, Guy put the stack back and headed for the ICU.

He found the man in room C. There wasn't much to see. Nepom was hooked up to a heart monitor, IV, respirator. Bandages covered his face and head, and his ribs had been taped.

There wasn't much hope, but he was glad to see Rachel had been so thorough. Everything that could have been done had been done. What he didn't see on the chart was that Nepom's family had been contacted.

After putting the chart back, Guy returned to admitting one more.

Karen gave him the rest of the night's paperwork, and he headed for his office and another cup of coffee.

He flipped through more notes. Damn. Rachel and Amy must have stitched, sewn, patched, splinted and put casts on nearly a hundred people since the storm started.

The name on the next report stopped him cold. Heather Corrigan. He did a quick check on her vital statistics: age eighteen, blond hair, no wedding ring. It was the Heather he knew. His stepdaughter. And she was dead.

Guy put the papers down on his desk and closed his eyes. Heather was supposed to be in Europe with his ex-wife. What was she doing here? Pregnant?

He focused his gaze with some difficulty, but as he

read, the words became horrifyingly clear. Preeclampsia. Heather was healthy, strong. For God's sake, she was only eighteen. And she'd died in his E.R. What the hell had Rachel done?

He picked up the phone with shaking fingers and dialed.

"Hi. You've reached Dr. Rachel Browne. Leave your number at the beep."

"Dr. Browne, this is Guy Giroux. Pick up the phone. Right now." He sat stiffly, a well of anger making it difficult to breathe, then slammed the receiver down when she didn't answer. He stared blankly at his desk for a moment, then pounded his fist on it so hard his pen holder fell over.

Rising slowly, Guy put on his coat, retrieved Heather's chart and headed for his car. He needed to talk to Dr. Browne—now.

CHAPTER TWO

THE DRIVE TO RACHEL'S did nothing to calm Guy's mind. He wavered between the respect he had for her as a doctor and the pain and rage he felt as a parent. He simply didn't understand how she could have been so incompetent.

His tires squealed as he came to a stop in her driveway, and once the keys were out of the ignition he was heading for her front door.

He rang the bell several times, then beat on the wood with his fists, almost hitting Rachel as the door suddenly flew open.

"What is it?"

Guy's tirade stopped before he was even able to start it. Dr. Rachel Browne, aka the Iron Lady, well known for her strict code of ethics and her somewhat aloof manner at the hospital, stood before him in a loose robe and tiny, see-through red nightie.

"Put your eyes back in their sockets, Guy, and tell me why you're waking me up two hours after I got off the seventeen-hour shift from hell?"

He tore his eyes away from the vision she presented and looked straight into her eyes. "What the hell happened in there last night?"

"What are you talking about?"

"Heather Corrigan. Healthy eighteen-year-old. And she's dead, Rachel."

Rachel blinked at him as if his words weren't English, as if she didn't know she'd killed a girl in his E.R. Killed—

"I'm sorry I didn't get the full report to you, Guy, but the girl had severe preeclampsia. I did everything possible to save her."

"Everything possible," he said, not believing that for a minute. "Where the hell was Williams?"

Rachel folded her robe tightly around her and slowly tied the knot in front. "There was only one OB on last night, and she was in the middle of a C-section with complications."

He knew he was scaring her, that her step backward was a precursor to slamming the door in his face, but there had to be something she'd missed. Something she could have done.

"Guy? What's going on?"

He focused on her face, realized his vision was blurry with tears. "She's…she was my stepdaughter."

Rachel's eyes closed for a long moment, and when she opened them she touched his arm. "Oh my God. I'm so sorry."

"Damn it, Rachel, she was always perfectly healthy. There's no reason this should have happened."

"She hadn't seen a doctor in a long time. No prenatal care at all. By the time she came in, her blood pressure was through the roof, the baby was almost dead. Guy, it was too late."

He swallowed, leaned against the doorframe. Blinked

his eyes clear. "I don't understand any of this. She was supposed to be in Europe with her mother."

"Why don't you come in. Sit down."

He shook his head. "I'm sorry. I'm sure you did everything. I just—"

"Of course."

"Go back to sleep. You must be tired."

"Are you sure you ought to be driving? With all the storm damage—"

"I'm fine. Sorry to have bothered you." He turned and walked to his car, wishing like hell he could blame her. Blame anyone except himself.

RACHEL WATCHED as Guy got into his Range Rover, worried that he'd do something crazy, get distracted. Just plain run off the road.

Heather Corrigan had been his stepdaughter. She could hardly believe it even now, but why would he lie about something so awful?

Guy pulled out of her driveway too quickly. When he jerked to a stop, she saw him wipe his face with his hand, and when he started up again, he was moving at a much saner pace. Only when he turned the corner, out of her view, did her focus shift to her street. Tousled and windblown for sure, it still had the peaceful mien that had drawn her here in the first place.

There were mostly two-story houses with manicured lawns. Bikes, ten-speed and trainers, leaned against garage doors or lay on the sidewalk, making it difficult for the mailman.

She'd been so drawn here, and yet she'd never felt

truly at home. Her night shifts, her single status. She was the odd duck, the silent stranger her neighbors nodded to when they couldn't avoid her gaze.

Exhaustion washed over her, and she wasn't quite sure whether it was the night before or the thought of the night ahead that made her so weary. Poor Guy. She'd had no idea. Yeah, she'd heard he'd been married before, but that was about the extent of her knowledge of his personal life.

The man was a hell of an administrator and an even better trauma surgeon. She was lucky to work with him.

But he was also terribly attractive, and not just because of his good looks. He pulled at her in a way that was too scary to examine closely. So she didn't. She avoided him by working nights most of the time. By never letting down her guard. By being a doctor first, and a woman a distant second.

She closed her door, debating whether to get a glass of orange juice, but her body led her to the bedroom and her Egyptian-cotton sheets. To sleep.

GUY DIDN'T GET BACK to his office and privacy for two hours. The longest two hours he'd ever spent.

It was just that he had to know. For certain. So he'd gone to the morgue. In that cold room, with the sterile sinks and the gleaming drawers, he'd found her. Death had changed her, stiffened her soft features, made her face a mask. But it was Heather. God, what had she done to her hair? It was short, uneven, as if cut by ragged scissors without a mirror.

He stood there for a long time, wishing he could remember some prayers. Finally he spoke, quietly, hoping someone, something, listened.

It was over now, and he knew for sure. After he put all the paperwork on Heather in front of him, he sat down behind his desk, sinking into the fine leather, and closed his eyes. Memories of Heather laughing, braiding her hair, begging him for a Madonna album despite the adult lyrics. He'd only had her for four years. Four years of emergency calls, late-night surgeries, missed school plays, forgotten birthdays. He'd been as lousy a stepparent as he'd been a husband. But he'd loved Heather. More than her mother, at the end, although that was no one's fault but his own.

He'd never blamed Tammy for leaving him. She had every right, and in fact, she'd probably stayed too long. His damn job. That was what she'd always called it. His damn job. And it had given him the only real satisfaction in his life.

He wasn't meant to be married, but the lesson had been learned the hard way. With other people's pain. And now, Heather was gone.

Guy hadn't known she was pregnant, or even that she'd had a boyfriend, a lover. He'd lost touch, and whose fault was that?

It took him a moment to locate Tammy's number in his Rolodex. She was living in Bordeaux, France, away with husband number three, studying art and learning to cook. Last time they'd talked, she'd sounded happy.

He got through after dialing all those numbers, and Tammy's voice sounded as if she were in the next room, not overseas.

"Bonjour."

"Tammy."

There was a pause, long and static-free. "Guy." She always used the French pronunciation. "To what do I owe this honor?"

He swallowed, picked up his pen and squeezed it. "I don't know how to… Oh hell, Tammy… Heather."

"What about Heather?"

He closed his eyes. "I'm sorry, Tammy. She's dead."

Nothing. No sound. No sharp cry, no keening wail. Just perfect silence.

"If this is a joke—"

"It's not. I wish it were."

Then came the sound of pain, and it was as terrible as anything he'd heard in all the years he'd been telling parents about their children, husbands about their wives… This was his grief, and her grief, and it was too real. It hurt like hot metal in his gut, like a gunshot wound.

"How?" Tammy said, her voice slurred.

"I didn't even know she was pregnant."

"What? What are you talking about? Heather's not pregnant. She's with her father. With Walter. In Los Angeles."

"No, she's not. She's here, in Courage Bay. I think—" He stopped. Swallowed. "I think she was trying to find me."

"Wait a minute. This makes no sense. I spoke to her two weeks ago, and she said everything was fine. That she was in L.A., that Walter was at the office, but that she would tell him hello."

Guy ran a hand over his face. "So you had no idea where she was? Who she was with?"

"No."

"Tammy—"

"Wait, stop right there. Don't you dare use that tone with me, not now. Not when…"

He listened to her weep and cursed himself for being an insensitive fool. "We should call Walter. Find out what he knows."

She sniffed. "Yes, right. But she was really pregnant?"

"She had a baby boy."

"Oh, God."

"And, I'm sorry, Tammy, but he's not doing all that well."

"What do you mean?"

"I'm not sure, except that he has jaundice and his blood pressure isn't stable."

"What do you mean, you're not sure? You're a doctor, for God's sake—that's all you've ever cared about. And now your grandchild is ill and you don't know why?"

Guy's first thought was that the boy wasn't his grandchild, but he said nothing. His second thought was that he was a complete ass. "I'm sorry. I've been having a tough time with this, too. I'm going from here to the NICU."

"I'm going to call Walter. And then I'll get on a plane. Please, Guy. You have to take care of the baby. Please."

"Of course."

She wept quietly for another moment. "I have to clear things with Ted. He's got this… It doesn't matter. I'll be there as soon as I can."

"You have my cell. Call me if you need me."

"Thank you."

He heard her hang up, and he listened to the dial tone for a second, then put his phone in the cradle. He had to go see the baby, make sure everything was being done to save him. A baby boy that Heather would never know. Who the hell was the father, and where had he been last night? Where had he been during the whole pregnancy?

A knock jerked him out of his thoughts and his sister, Natalie, poked her head in. "Can I come in?"

He nodded.

She stepped into his office, closing the door behind her. Six years his junior, she bore the distinctive Giroux high cheekbones and dark eyes. Natalie was a burn specialist, and their brother, Alec, worked in the E.R. with Guy. "I heard about Heather, Guy. I'm so terribly sorry."

"Does everybody know?"

She smiled the way she did with her patients. Kind, concerned, ready to listen. "This isn't L.A. County General, Guy. These things get around pretty fast."

His head dropped into his hands. "She deserved better, Nat. I don't know how it happened."

She walked behind him and massaged his tense shoulder muscles. "Things happen, Guy. Mom—Dad. You have to believe there's a reason."

"Don't get all metaphysical on me. Does Alec know yet?"

"He's already left for Cabo with Janice and the kids. But I'll call him. Let him know what's going on. I know he liked Heather a great deal. We both did. She was a sweet girl."

Guy's throat tightened, and he had to change the subject before he made a fool of himself. His sister had recently married the city's fire chief, Dan Egan. "How are things with you and Dan?"

Natalie walked to his side and smiled. "Really good. Thanks. In fact, why don't you come for dinner tomorrow night?"

Guy appreciated the invitation. He liked Dan, and was happy that Nat had found herself a good man. Both his siblings had been through so much in the last year, and yet they'd come out stronger, better. In love. And he'd never felt so distant from them. "Thanks, Nat, but I'm going to stick close to the hospital. I'll take a rain check."

"Anytime, big brother."

"I'm going to get to the bottom of this. I swear it."

Her beeper went off. Natalie sighed, patted his still-tense shoulders and headed for the door. "You're an incredible doctor, Guy, and a pretty decent man. I know you'll do the right thing, whatever it is." With a final smile, she left his office, closing the door behind her.

CALLIE BAKER SET ASIDE the damage report and her master list of what had to be done to get the hospital back to perfect working order, even though she hadn't even started on the delegation sheet. It was time for rounds.

She knew most chiefs of staff didn't go on master rounds, but for her it was a sacred ritual. Although she could only manage it once a week, twice if she was lucky, it was the one duty that kept her heart and her mind completely focused on who she was and what her job was all about.

Above all else, she was a doctor, and she liked to think she was a damn good one. The administrative duties would swamp her if she let them, and that wasn't going to happen as long as she had something to say about it.

It had taken her a long time and a hard road to get where she was, and one of the key ingredients to her success was her ability to see the big picture while never losing sight of the details.

Before she left the office, she stopped in the small restroom and made sure she was put together. After a quick application of lip gloss and a readjustment of the hummingbird pin on her jacket lapel, she straightened her white coat and headed out to the front lines.

Everything went according to plan until she hit the ICU. Callie read through Bruce Nepom's chart three times. His prognosis wasn't good. In fact, it was a miracle that he was still breathing. His injuries had been severe, especially the cranial damage. That's what had caught her attention. Something didn't fit. A deep, focused trauma at the back of the skull.

She looked at the man, swathed in bandages. His blood pressure was so low as to be a hint instead of a statement, and she knew it was only a matter of time. A short time. She wondered why he was here alone.

After making a note on the chart that she wanted to be updated on his progress, Callie continued her rounds. Bruce Nepom's injuries lingered in her mind, however. A fuzzy question that had to be answered.

RACHEL WOKE UP SUDDENLY at two-thirty from a dream. Guy Giroux had been to her house. But unlike the real event, this time he'd come in and he'd wept like a child. In her dream she'd tried to comfort him, but her own discomfort made her awkward and jerky. He didn't seem to notice, but Rachel was beyond mortified. It was like seeing the man naked, or walking in on him making love.

Guy had a place, and it was at the hospital. He had a role, and that was as her boss. Anything that disturbed that picture was uncomfortable and to be avoided at all costs.

Only, the picture *was* disturbed now. Guy had lost his stepdaughter. Someone he cared about, loved. He'd been married, which Rachel had known but never thought about, and there had been a little girl in his life. It was altogether too personal.

At work, Rachel was an attending physician and little else. She listened to her staff, joked with them, even went for the occasional drink after a tough night. But she kept her private life to herself.

She'd learned early that, as a doctor, emotional objectivity was a good thing. Not that she didn't care what happened to her patients. In fact, that's where all her nurturing went—to the people who needed her. The truth was, she was *too* emotional. Things affected her deeply, and she cared way too much when confronted with pain and suffering she could do nothing about.

Rachel had been that way all her life, and it had made for a roller-coaster puberty. Her friends' lives all became larger than life, their joys were hers to share, and their pain cut her to the core.

Her decision to become a doctor was born from a

deep need to make things better. Not just for others, but for herself. She couldn't stand feeling helpless.

In grade school she'd had a dear, wonderful friend. Molly had moved two houses down when they were both in fourth grade, and it had been love at first sight. They lived at each other's houses, played together constantly, dreamed big dreams. Molly was like a sister to Rachel, only they fought less.

And at fifteen, Molly got bone cancer. Two years later, she'd died, and Rachel had nearly gone with her, her grief was so consuming. Standing by, watching her friend's body waste away was the most excruciating experience of her life, and from that time on, nothing had swayed her from her course.

It was in medical school that Rachel realized she couldn't help anyone if she was engulfed in grief herself, so she decided she simply wouldn't let it in. It was as if she'd created an invisible bubble around herself, and nothing came through.

Nothing.

The strategy had worked so well it almost scared her, whenever she let herself think about it. Because there was one problem: she'd never been able to figure out a way to let the positive emotions enter through the barricade.

Not that she was unhappy. The satisfaction she got from her job was deep and fine. But was it enough?

Waking up alone, going to sleep alone, cooking for one… It fell short. Not short enough to make her give up her career or even curtail her hours. If she ever did meet anyone, he'd have to deal with that, or hit the road.

For some unknown reason, she thought of Guy again.

She needed to think of him as her boss, not a man. A really attractive man.

That was one road she wasn't going down. Nope. No way. He was off-limits. Completely and utterly. He was the reason she preferred the night shift and why she did all she could to keep their communication on paper.

Rachel threw the covers back and headed for the shower. Her shift didn't start until nine, but she had shopping to do, some calls to make. And she wanted to get to the hospital early to review her paperwork and check on Heather Corrigan's baby boy.

CHAPTER THREE

ELEANOR FITZ, the charge nurse in the NICU, wasn't someone Guy new well. He dealt with her during administrative meetings and whenever a preemie was born in the E.R. They'd never talked, aside from work. He didn't understand his reticence to approach her now, and he pushed it aside, intent on seeing Heather's child.

When Eleanor saw him standing just inside the room, she seemed startled, but she quickly hid her surprise. "Dr. Giroux, how can I help you?"

He walked directly to the large sink and scrubbed his hands as if preparing for surgery. Then he draped a sterile mask around his neck and walked across the room to the nurses' station, his gaze sweeping the incubators, isolettes, infant warmers and bevy of monitors hooked up to the tiny charges. The other nurses, most of whom he recognized, were busy, and there were two fathers, one holding his child, the other looking desperately through an incubator at his.

"I'm looking for Heather Corrigan's baby," he said.

For a split second Eleanor's forehead creased, but perhaps he imagined it because when she smiled, she seemed all business. "He's right over here." Turning, she led him to the incubator at the far end of the room. Both a heart and a respiratory monitor were connected, and when he got closer, he saw an IV tube inserted into the hand of an incredibly tiny, very yellow baby.

"What's his condition?"

The nurse didn't even pluck the chart from the corner of the incubator. "He's doing better than he was, but that's not saying much. Very low blood pressure. You can see his jaundice is advanced and his kidney is only at ten percent. There's still a lot we don't know. His blood work isn't finished."

Guy stopped himself before he snapped at the woman in his frustration. "Please call the lab immediately and have his bloods done, stat."

"Yes, Doctor," she said, the words an unasked question.

"This is my stepdaughter's child. I'd like to be informed immediately of any changes. You have my beeper, I assume."

"Yes, Doctor," she said, and it was if she had changed into another person. Softer. Sympathetic.

He wanted to make her leave, and he could have with a glance, but he didn't. The child deserved all the sympathy in the world, considering his stepgrandfather.

"I'll get right on it, Doctor," Eleanor said, stepping aside. "I'll leave you two to get acquainted."

He nodded, his gaze on the boy.

"Doctor?"

He turned, surprised that the nurse was still there. "Yes."

"Does he have a name?"

Guy stared without seeing. Thought about his girl, the way her hair insisted on flying about in the most undisciplined manner, no matter how she tried to tame it. About the way her laugh made him smile, even when he was in the foulest mood. "Heath," he said. He looked at the baby once more. "His name is Heath Corrigan."

RACHEL WAS STILL a little stunned at the storm damage she'd seen on her errands. Roofs had blown off, trees had toppled, electrical wires had been ripped from their housings. It was amazing the E.R. hadn't been ten times as busy.

She'd finished her grocery shopping, gone to the post office and to the dry cleaners. Tonight would end her graveyard shift, and the day after tomorrow she would begin days. It wasn't an easy transition to make, not only because of her body clock, but because of the social aspects of the day shift.

There were more patients, more interactions, more staff. She'd be doing rounds with Guy, seeing him in the call room, in the lounge. It was also time for her yearly review, and while she felt confident her performance was up to par, she didn't like the fact that Guy had so much power over her.

Not that she hadn't had supervisors and bosses before. She'd done her residency at Baylor in Houston, and they were notorious for their brutal reviews, but no one had ever flustered her the way Guy did. For all her expertise at disassociating her emotions, she failed miserably when she was around him.

She'd given up denying her attraction to him. It was there. Big time. But just because she felt it didn't mean she had to act on it.

She just wished it would go away—that she could cure her attraction like a headache and be done with it.

And now, given his grief at the loss of Heather, she needed to be extra attentive, more personal, giving.

Okay, she wanted to be those things because no one should have to go through his pain, but the territory was dangerous and she had to be so very careful not to let him get too close. Not to let her guard down.

Once Rachel arrived at the hospital, she headed straight for the NICU.

In the elevator to the fourth floor, two nurses joined her. Rachel smiled at them and stood to one side. Of course she knew them both—they worked in cardiology—but not well.

"I know," Cathy said, her voice just above a whisper, yet clear as a bell to Rachel. "I couldn't believe it. His own stepdaughter."

"I heard he was just devastated," Ilene whispered back.

The elevator stopped on Two, and the nurses left without a backward glance. Rachel sighed. Courage Bay was a small hospital, and rumors raced through it like a fire. That was another reason she had no intention of letting Guy's situation get to her. Nothing went unnoticed around here, and she would rather die than be the subject of staff gossip. It was enough that she'd earned herself the nickname of the Iron Lady. No one had ever said it to her face, but she'd heard it in the lounge, even on the floor. Better she should be known by that moniker than as a soft touch.

At the fourth floor, she headed toward the NICU, but as she passed the big windows, she came to an abrupt halt. Guy Giroux, her tough-as-nails boss, sat in a rock-ing chair, a sterile mask covering the lower half of his face, a tiny bundle, still hooked up to an array of mon-itors, cradled in his arms.

A wave of compassion swept through her, as strong as the winds that had toppled the trees last night. Without her permission, tears filled her eyes and she had to blink them away as she struggled to regain her composure.

This wasn't the plan. She hadn't even spoken to the man and she was getting blubbery. This never happened to her. Not anymore.

She got a grip on herself, straightened her shoulders and headed into the room, stopping to wash her hands and grab a mask before she walked over to him.

Guy didn't look up. She doubted he knew she was there, the way he was watching the child.

Oh, God, the baby was so small and so jaundiced. Her gaze went to the monitors, and she was immediately concerned about both the BP and the heart rhythm.

"Hello, Rachel," Guy said.

She smiled, but her body was almost rigid with con-trol. "Hello, Doctor. I came up to see how the baby is doing."

"I wish it was better," he said, and that's when he looked up at her.

It was as if she were staring at a new man. All she could see were his eyes, but the change in him was pal-pable. Guy had always been compassionate—that was one of the things that made him such a good doctor—but this was…different. There was a softness she would never have guessed, right there in his dark gaze.

"What can I do?" she asked.

He hesitated. "Before we get into that, I want to apologize for this morning. I had no business barging in—"

She held up her hand, her face filling with heat as she remembered her outfit, or lack of one. "It's not a problem. I'm sorry I didn't finish up the paperwork yesterday. I came in early to do just that, but if I can help here, I'd like to."

He smiled. Not that she could see his lips curve through the mask, but the corners of his eyes crinkled. "I know beyond any shadow of a doubt that you did everything possible for Heather. I'm still stunned about all this. I spoke to her mother. Seems she thought Heather was in Los Angeles with her father."

"Oh, no."

"Tammy didn't even know about the pregnancy." His gaze went back to the boy. "This little guy had no help coming into this world. No prenatal care, no grandparents. I just don't understand. This wasn't like Heather. She's always been a good kid."

In the two years she'd been at Courage Bay Hospital, she'd never had such a personal conversation with Guy. Her first instinct was to get out, go back to the world she knew, but she could tell he wasn't finished. That he needed to talk.

So she walked over to an empty incubator and grabbed the rocking chair positioned next to it. She placed it close to Guy's chair. Settling into it, she crossed her legs and leaned back. "Tell me about her."

Guy touched the baby's tiny arm with his index finger. "I only had Heather for four years. Her mother and

I got divorced when she was thirteen. She was bright. Heather, I mean. Inquisitive. I'd hoped that someday she'd become interested in medicine, but back then, all she cared about were boys and music, music and boys. Oh, I forgot clothes. Those were big, too."

"She sounds like a typical teenager."

"In a lot of ways, she was." Guy looked at her, although Rachel had the feeling he wasn't really seeing her. "She loved to sail. I suppose that's where we spent most of our time together. I was always getting home after she went to bed, leaving before she woke up."

"That's the doctor's curse."

"It cursed that marriage, all right. But I learned my lesson. Never again. I wasn't there for either of them. They needed me, but I didn't give much of a damn. Tammy…"

She didn't press him to finish the sentence. In fact, she didn't want to hear the rest. His confession was hitting her in a place long buried. The two of them were so alike. At least Rachel had never made the mistake of getting married. She knew it would be just as Guy said. She wouldn't be there in a way a wife or mother needed to be.

"Tammy's in France, but she's going to get here as soon as she can. I still haven't connected with Heather's father. I left two messages, but the number I have may be old."

"Do you think he knew what was going on?"

Guy shook his head. "I never cared much for Walter. The idiot. He was unfocused and a wastrel, but I never imagined he was this negligent." His voice hardened into something Rachel recognized a lot more than his previous gentle cadence. "I'm going to find out exactly what he knew, and when. And how he could have let this happen. I blame him for Heather's death."

His head bowed a little farther, as if she wasn't there. Rachel barely heard his next words, they were whispered so softly. "And myself."

"Guy, you've been divorced from Tammy for how long?"

He didn't answer for a long moment. "Five years."

"And the last time you checked, Heather was supposed to be with her mother in Europe?"

He nodded. "Yeah. The last time I checked. Which was months ago."

"I know this is hard, but don't borrow any more grief than you already have. There's no way you could have known that Heather wasn't with her parents. Or that she was pregnant. Her own mother didn't know."

"That doesn't absolve me, and you know it. But I'll tell you one thing, Rachel—I'm going to get to the bottom of this. And I'm going to make sure Heath is taken care of. In every way."

"Heath?"

"After his mom," Guy said, rocking the baby gently. "He needs to get better. I have to figure out exactly what's going on here and fix it."

"Then let me help."

His chair stopped. "How?"

"I'll go to the lab and I'll go over the reports with a fine-tooth comb. Let me call Tim Burns…get him in here."

"He's on vacation."

Rachel knew the neonatologist was away, but she

also knew that he was only in Palm Springs, and that if he understood the situation, he'd get back here, pronto. She also knew the specialists on staff were perfectly capable of handling preemies and all the problems that went with them, but Burns was the best. And he was Guy's friend. "Let me worry about that." She stood up, put the rocker back. "I'll page you as—"

The baby's heart monitor went off that second, and even though every instinct she had was to rush in to see what was wrong and what she could do, she stepped back as the team swarmed around Guy and the incubator.

After a few moments, she realized Heath had gone into arrhythmia, and the medical staff had to do some pretty fancy footwork to stabilize him. Which they did, thank God. Now it was a matter of keeping him stabilized, and that's something she could help with.

Guy was standing at the foot of the incubator, his skin paler than she'd ever seen it before. She touched his arm. "I'll call," Rachel said softly.

He barely acknowledged her.

She wished she could do more. Say something, be someone who could ease his torment. But she couldn't.

GUY WENT TO HIS OFFICE and sat down, his head still muzzy with so many thoughts. Heath was stable for the moment, but the information Rachel had gotten from the lab strongly indicated that the boy had a genetic problem, perhaps Noonan's syndrome, though more tests had to be run.

The thing was, he knew for a fact that there was no indication of Noonan's in Walter's or Tammy's background. So if that was the final diagnosis, the disorder had to have been transmitted through the father.

Noonan's. It was a relatively common birth defect, and Guy had seen his share of cases. Some severe, some blessedly mild. From Heath's current physical symptoms, the slight webbing on his neck, his low-set ears, it didn't appear that he had severe Noonan's, but there were still heart tests, the karyotype analysis and the genetic tests for mutation in the PTPN11 gene. What no one knew yet was if the boy would be developmentally challenged, which happened in about a fourth of the cases.

Nothing was more important than finding Heath's father and getting his medical history. If the same genetic testing could be done on the father, Heath's chances for survival would be greatly enhanced, but Guy didn't have a clue where to begin.

Rachel was checking into Heather's belongings, and he'd put in four calls to Walter. Guy wanted to kill the son of a bitch for not calling him back.

He wanted coffee, but he didn't have the wherewithal to get up and get it. He didn't like asking Connie, but today would have to be the exception to the rule. Leaning over his desk, hardly looking at the paperwork he couldn't deal with yet, he buzzed his secretary.

"Yes, Doctor?"

"I hate to ask, but could you make me a pot of coffee?"

Connie chuckled. "It's already made, just five minutes ago. So you just sit right there, and I'll bring you a cup."

Guy smiled. "Thank you."

"No sweat."

He sat back in his chair, knowing full well why there was a fresh pot of coffee made. Everyone in the hospital, including Connie, knew about Heather. About Heath. And they would all be solicitous and pitying and it would be a nightmare on top of a nightmare for Guy.

Putting his hand on the back of his neck, he rubbed the tense muscles as Connie entered his office, tapping first, as she always did. She looked bright and sunny today, her dress a brilliant red that made her café au lait skin appear smooth and vibrant, belying her fifty-plus years. She'd been with Guy for the past three years, and their relationship was one of businesslike companionability. He appreciated the fact that he never had to ask for anything twice. Connie was proud of her work, and it showed.

Today, however, her concern wasn't about hospital matters, but him, and he could see it in her eyes, the way her smile was filled with concern. "How are you?" she asked.

"As well as could be expected."

She nodded, then disappeared into his call room. It held only a bed, a locker, a small radio and of course, his coffee supplies. When Connie reappeared, she held a steaming mug, which she put in front of him.

"Thank you."

"Hold on," she said, then she hurried out of the office, leaving the door slightly ajar.

It wasn't but a moment till she was back, this time with a plate. "I made some spiced pumpkin bread last night before we lost power. Luckily, it baked all the way through. I know it's one of your favorites."

He couldn't tell her that the thought of food made his stomach turn. "Thanks, Connie."

"And I don't care if you're not hungry. You eat a piece. You need to be at your best for that little boy."

"So it's all over the hospital, is it?"

"Of course." She sat down across from his desk, in one of the two brown leather wing chairs. "Which means what it means. What I want to know is how I can help."

Guy sipped some coffee. It was perfect, just as he'd expected. "There's nothing to be done, except your usual excellence. It might be a little tougher in the next few days because of the storm. I'll need an updated schedule of the staff. Has everyone checked in?"

"Yes, sir. Only Williams still can't get in. But he thinks he'll be cleared out by tonight."

He nodded, thinking about his team. They were good. In fact, it was the best E.R. in the state, as far as he was concerned. Recently they'd handled things even metropolitan hospitals never saw. He thought of his brother, Alec, and how brilliant he'd been during the virus outbreak last summer. Then there had been the weather anomalies, the fires. It had been the most hectic year Courage Bay had known, and Guy's E.R. had done more than anyone could have expected. "I may have to leave town for a few days," he said, "so we'll need a working plan for a week without me."

"Of course," Connie said.

"The baby isn't out of the woods, not by a long shot. I want—" He stopped, startled at the direction of his thoughts, at the depth of his emotions. "I want to spend as much time as I can with him, until he is."

Connie tilted her head a bit to the right. "You're family. It's only natural."

But it wasn't natural. It was nothing like Guy. Why he cared so much, why Heath's condition meant so much to him was a puzzle that shook him. He'd had other family members in trouble before. His own mother, for God's sake. He'd been there for her, as much as he could be after the car accident that had killed his father and eventually taken her life, but he'd never felt this much at sea.

It was unprecedented and the stupid thing was, Heath wasn't even his blood. It didn't matter. He would do whatever it took to take care of the boy.

"Is that it?" Connie asked. "I feel like I should do more. Help more."

He knew just what she was talking about, but he couldn't think of a thing. As long as she kept him and the team organized, that was all he could ask.

As long as Rachel was there…

What a thought to have about Rachel Browne. Up until today, he would have said she was a colleague, one of his staff. He noticed her beauty, of course, but since very early on, there had been no question of crossing the line, of being anything more than her boss. And yet today, he'd acted as if she was more. A friend. Someone to turn to.

It was official. His world had turned upside down. There was a life depending on him that hadn't been there yesterday, and for once, he had no excuses to back out. No other priorities. And where just a few short hours ago it seemed he was in this alone, he now had a friend. Rachel.

Go figure.

CHAPTER FOUR

RACHEL HELD the plastic bin tightly, as if it would drop any second. It wasn't a special bin, except that inside it were all the worldly goods of an eighteen-year-old who'd died on Rachel's watch.

She'd gone over the medical procedures in her mind a hundred times, reread her notes six times, maybe seven. And still, she couldn't think of a thing she'd have done differently. She'd taken extraordinary measures to save Heather's life. And still, she'd failed.

It happened. Rachel had also heard that Bruce Nepom had died this morning, which didn't make things better. God, she'd tried so hard. The damage that had been done to that man's skull...

She reached her office and kicked the door shut behind her. Then she put the bin on the table, wincing at the grooves embedded in her palms.

Going through Heather's things was a breach of protocol, but in this case, it was done out of kindness. If there was anything disturbing in the meager belongings, she wanted to see it first, then tell Guy. Since the death wasn't suspicious, there would be no police involvement. And since Guy was acting as next of kin, there was no harm here, only help.

Heather's coat was on top. It wasn't in good repair, and there were stains on the poor-quality wool. The blue color had faded, leaving it washed out and sad looking. There was one piece of paper in her pocket, and on it were two phone numbers. Rachel recognized the one for Courage Bay Hospital. The other had a 213 prefix. Los Angeles. She carefully put the paper, wrinkled and still a bit damp, in her jacket pocket.

After folding the coat, Rachel picked up Heather's dress. Another thrift-store bargain, she imagined. Yellow, with little green flowers. No pockets. Next was Heather's purse. It was a large cotton tote, with lots of pockets inside. Unfortunately, they didn't hold much of consequence—breath mints, a hairbrush, dark glasses, a faded ticket stub to a movie. But then Rachel found a small notebook. She opened it to the first page. The handwriting was small, tight.

I'm here, finally. Away from all of them. Safe. Well, not now, because he's not here. But he'll be back soon, and then it will be dinner and maybe we'll watch an old movie on his crappy TV. I won't care because we'll be together. It was so easy. I still can't get over that. Mom didn't even check. Dad was busy with his bimbo of the month. And I disappeared, like on that TV show where someone's there one second, and gone the next. Only, no one's looking for me. And it feels...

Rachel turned the page, but it was a new entry, written with a different pen. Leaning back in her chair, Ra-

chel wondered if she should go immediately to find
Guy, but something kept her in her seat. Fear. Protectiveness. She turned back to the book.

*We went to his friend's house last night, but I don't
remember all that much. I got totally wasted, and
this chick, Perry, scored some Ecstasy, which I'd
never done before. Mixed with the Southern Comfort, it was so cool. I like his friends, although
Perry's boyfriend scared me a little when we were
in the kitchen together. He touched me, but then
Perry came in so it was cool again. After, S and I
made love until, like, four in the morning. Then he
went to sleep, and I think if it had been quieter, I
would have, too, but the sirens went on and on,
and then there was this helicopter. I could see the
light, really bright, on the walls. They're cracked
between the posters, and the paint is really
chipped. I wonder if this is where we'll always
live, or if he'll get that job, and then we can move
somewhere nice, where the carpet isn't stained,
and we can have a washer and dryer, 'cause I hate
going to that skeezy Laundromat. We'd have a
new bed, too, one that didn't make my back ache
every morning. And I could buy new sheets and a
comforter and stuff. I really want to decorate my
way for a change, and have all the money in the
world to buy whatever I want. He says we'll have
everything, and I believe him. I just have to wait.
But I don't know how long to wait. I said I should
look for a job, but he got really pissed, and so I*

didn't mention it again. He's going to take care of me. He promised. I know he will, 'cause he loves me. More than anything on earth. He loves ME.

Rachel's chest constricted with pain for this child. She did a little elementary math. Heather had to have been pregnant nine months ago, yet she didn't appear to be when she'd written this. How long ago would that have been?

Flipping through the pages, Rachel saw that the entries were made in different colors of ink, mostly black, but some in blue, red, and a few in purple. The handwriting got even smaller toward the end, which was probably where Rachel should have looked to start with.

She found the last entry more than three-quarters of the way through the small notebook.

I've been gone for almost a week. Does he think I'm dead? Hit by a car, or mugged, or maybe he thinks I had the baby? I still don't understand what happened. How it all went to hell. He loved me. He told me so over and over. Loved me, and he would take care of me, and take care of our baby. And then he wouldn't let me out of the house. I thought it was because he was worried about me. But even when I wanted to go, when I felt fine, he kept me locked up. Got mean. He wouldn't talk to me, wouldn't explain. And when I tried so hard to understand, he just hit me. It hurt so bad.

And then he left, and it was three days before he got back. I tried to get out, but he'd done something to the door. He took his cell phone and didn't leave me any money, so what was I supposed to do?

And then, yesterday, when he was gone again, that guy from the apartment came. I couldn't believe it at first, but then I started screaming and I didn't stop until he'd gotten the door open. He didn't want to help me, but I guess he felt sorry for the baby. He got me out, took me to the bus station, gave me some money. And now I'm waiting for the bus.

The scariest part is the headaches. They've gotten so much worse. The baby keeps kicking so I haven't slept, and I have to keep going to the bathroom.

I don't want to call my mom or dad. But Guy will help. He was the best, when he was there. I wonder if he's forgotten me. I remember the times we went on the boat together. That was cool. I wish he could have been my real father. Then he might have stayed home more, and we could have been a real family. I guess I'd

That was it. The last entry. Rachel closed the book and got up, put the lid back on the plastic bin and headed for Guy's office.

Connie was on the phone in the outer office, but she waved at Rachel to go inside.

Rachel knocked lightly, then opened the door enough

to see Guy at his desk. His head rested on his hands, his shoulders were slumped, and he didn't look up.

"Yes, Connie."

"It's me," she said. "May I come in?"

He raised his head, and smiled at her. God, he looked like hell, red-rimmed eyes, his dark hair unkempt and spiky. For the first time she could remember, Guy looked every one of his forty-three years. But in his sad smile was a welcome that she took to heart.

"I have something," she said, holding up the notebook. "It was in Heather's things."

He changed instantly, becoming fully alert. The intelligence that made him so appealing lit up his eyes.

She went to his desk and handed him the book. He took it anxiously, but when he opened it randomly, somewhere in the middle, he glanced up from the small script to her.

"I'll leave you," she said. "You should read it."

"Have you?"

"Just a bit," she told him, embarrassed. "I hoped there would be something obvious."

He nodded, looked down at the page again. "Are you on shift?"

"Yes."

"Are there patients?"

"Yes. Nothing too urgent."

His gaze met hers. "Come back."

She took in a great breath of air, trying to steady herself, to mentally step back, get some room, but there was no place she could go. He needed someone, and she was it. "As soon as I can."

"Thank you," he said.

She didn't reply, but at the door she turned back to ask, "Have you eaten?"

"Now you're sounding like Connie."

"Good. Someone needs to look after you."

"I'm fine."

"And the baby?"

Guy didn't speak, and his gaze went to the window. "He's in trouble. I was just up there. They think it's Noonan's syndrome, but they're not sure. We need to find the father."

"Maybe that will help," she said, looking at the notebook.

"I hope so. I still haven't heard from Walter."

"I have to go," Rachel said, "but I'll be back as soon as I can. And Guy?"

"Yeah?"

"I'm off tomorrow. After that, I switch to days. So whatever help I can offer, count on it."

His lips tightened, and he was staring at the window again. Rachel closed the door quietly behind her.

BY THE TIME Guy finished reading Heather's diary, it was nearly nine-thirty. He looked at his desk and saw the piles of reports neatly laid in his in-box. He hadn't even heard Connie come in or leave for the day.

When he rubbed his face, he was startled that his eyes, his cheeks were wet. He'd cried? God, he was falling apart. Everything felt surreal—Heather's death, this book of sorrows, Heath.

Heath.

He stood up, carefully putting Heather's notebook in his top drawer, and headed for the NICU. Again, the staff treated him diffidently. Gave him more room in the hallways, smiled with that tinge of sympathy that made him want to punch through a wall. He retreated into familiar behavior, acting as if nothing had happened, nodding but not speaking.

The elevator held only strangers, and for that Guy was grateful. On the fourth floor, he listened to the soft strains of Bach wafting beneath the bustle of nurses and orderlies. On this floor, aside from the NICU, was the nursery. If he walked to his left, he would see the healthy babies, the exultant parents. Just past the nursery was a waiting room, and then there was the delivery room.

He knew that Heather had been in the right place last night, and because of Rachel's deft handling of the delivery, Heath was alive today. And yet he couldn't help but wonder *what if.*

What if he'd called Heather more often? What if he'd paid attention? What if he hadn't been such a selfish prick for the last five years?

He felt the blood beneath his skin and was aware of his rapid heartbeat. His breath became shallow and harsh, and he ducked into the men's room. Alone, he went to the sink and threw cold water on his face. Tried for calm, settled for nonpsychotic.

He leaned on the granite counter, stared into his own wild eyes. He'd gone through the looking glass this morning, and it had just turned into a mirror again. He didn't like what he saw.

Who the hell was he? A doctor, but why? Did he even

care about the people he helped? Or was it all self-aggrandizement? Had he ever loved Tammy, or was it just that she was beautiful? That she thought he was God's gift? That she fit into the pretty little picture he'd created that represented his life. Only, where was the life part?

The moment he'd held that boy in his arms, the facade had shattered. But now that Guy was broken, what was he supposed to do about it? How was he going to pick up the pieces? That baby needed him, and he was useless. Stripped bare and without any of his shiny protective coating.

"Okay, Giroux. Get it together. This is *not* about you." He turned off the water, then dried his hands and face, balling the paper tightly before he threw it in the trash. Then he went to look in on his grandson.

As he walked into the unit, his gaze went to the far corner. Heath's incubator. And Rachel Browne.

Instantly, as if a switch had been flipped, his anger disappeared. Gone, just like that. He studied her. Her long, dark hair was pulled back into a neat ponytail that fell to the middle of her back. The white coat, prim, professional, hid the curves that had burned themselves into his brain. Her navy skirt came down to just above her knees, and below that were remarkable legs, the kind of legs that launched ships, that wars were fought over. Her shoes—black, with one-inch heels—were as perfectly groomed as the rest of her. That was Rachel. Always put together, always fresh and beautiful, even if she'd been working twenty-four hours straight.

She instilled confidence in her patients, had complete control of even the most complicated cases. And she never lost her cool. Altogether, she was an extraordinary doctor.

Right this second, he needed her, more desperately than he could ever remember needing a woman. But not for sex or even a kiss. He needed her to calm him. When Rachel was near, the world stopped caving in on him.

He went to the sink first and prepared himself to hold the baby. It was second nature, this washing routine. He'd done it so many times, hundreds, thousands, that it had become a ritual.

Rachel was looking at him when he turned toward Heath. God, her face. It was the best part of her, really. Incredibly large dark eyes, dark eyebrows, and lips painted a perfect red. She had a fascinating beauty, but more important, she was a born healer, in the best sense of the word. And in his eyes, that made her looks a detail. An afterthought.

That didn't mean he couldn't appreciate how attractive she was. He simply put her beauty in proper perspective.

"Guy," she said, her soft voice carrying clearly across the room.

He walked toward her, the stirrings of hope quickening his step.

"He's doing a little better," Rachel said. "He's been sleeping peacefully. No arrhythmia, and look—" she handed him the chart "—his kidney function is up."

Guy read everything, then reread it before he spoke. "He's still not out of the woods."

"No," Rachel said. "But what this tells me is that even if we don't find his father, we can get to the bottom of his condition. We'll find out everything. His blood work has gone to the lab in San Francisco."

He knew what that meant. DNA sequencing, as fast and as accurately as it could be done. It cost him a fortune and was worth every penny. But it still wasn't magic. Getting the results would take time. Time he could use finding the bastard that had impregnated his stepdaughter. "His name is Stan," he said. "I think he might still be in Los Angeles."

Rachel stepped closer and put her hand on his sleeve. "When's the last time you ate?"

"I don't know."

"Well then, here's what we're going to do. You're going to spend a few minutes looking at that beautiful boy. Then I'm going to take you down the street and force-feed you, if necessary." She caught his gaze. "We'll talk."

CHAPTER FIVE

RACHEL WALKED next to Guy, her hands in her coat pockets. As they approached the Courage Bay Bar and Grill, she slipped a glance his way, the light from a street lamp putting his features in sharp relief.

He didn't look like the Guy Giroux she was used to. His dark hair, thick and long enough to brush his collar, was mussed, and his strong jaw was darkened with a five o'clock shadow. His eyebrows, which would have been too bushy on a weaker face, made everything about his looks more interesting.

There was no disputing he was handsome. And tall. She guessed he was about six-three. At five-eight, she only reached his shoulders. And then there was his body. The man took care of himself, and didn't all the nurses and female doctors notice. Guy was often the subject of break-room gossip and wishful thinking.

In all the time she'd worked at the hospital, she'd never heard of him dating anyone on staff. Considering how small-town the E.R. was, that was a good thing. Nothing escaped their co-workers, and this innocent dinner would be no exception. Rachel didn't give a damn.

It was startling how affected Guy was by the loss of

his stepdaughter. He had clearly loved Heather, and his concern for the baby was as deep as a parent's.

It occurred to Rachel that she barely knew the man. She only knew the doctor. Which was exactly how it was supposed to be. Only, things had changed, and the man inside the black leather coat needed her. She couldn't bring Heather back, and she wasn't the best doctor for Heath. But she could be a friend.

They reached the door of the restaurant and Guy held it open for her. Inside, the cold of the January night disappeared. The familiar surroundings helped take the chill out of Rachel. Larry Goodman, the owner, was hosting this evening, and he greeted them both warmly, took their coats and led them to the dining room, to a back booth.

Like all the emergency personnel in town, Rachel came to the Bar and Grill more often than any other place. Aside from the convenient location, the restaurant had great food, the ambience was calming, and Larry and his wife, Louise, went to great lengths to take care of all the teams in the emergency-services district.

She scooted into the far seat of the booth, while Guy sat across from her. "Tea, please, Larry. Earl Grey."

Larry, who looked younger than his sixty-plus years, nodded and turned to Guy.

"Coffee."

"Be right back, folks. Tonight we have some great mesquite-smoked salmon, and the prime rib has been getting raves."

The minute they were alone, Guy pulled the little notebook out of his pocket and put it on the table.

Rachel's gaze moved back and forth between the diary and Guy, but he only stared at the book. She watched the play of candlelight on his face, the way the shadows made his eyebrows look even thicker, his lips look firm and cool.

"What did you read?" he asked, jarring her out of her reverie.

"Not much. The first two pages. The last."

Guy nodded. "She didn't mention his name for a while. I got the feeling she was scared that someone would find the diary, then find her."

Larry brought their drinks. Rachel ordered the salmon, and Guy chose chicken Dijon. Both of them asked for salads. Larry slipped away quietly, as if he understood this was not a night for catching up.

Guy pushed the book to the side then looked straight at her. "He held her prisoner there. Got her hooked on drugs, got her pregnant, then locked her away."

"Why? What was he after?"

He shook his head. "She was fooled for a long time. She thought he was in love with her, and even after he started hitting her, she didn't want to believe the truth. I don't think she even knew the truth."

"You said his name was Stan. No last name, I presume?"

"Nope."

Rachel pulled the paper out of her pocket and slid it across to him. "This was in her coat pocket."

After he picked it up, Guy was silent for a long time. "Why didn't she call me?" he said at last.

"I don't know. But maybe that other phone number will give us a lead."

Guy put the paper inside the small notebook and when he looked back at Rachel, he was smiling. "Us?"

She felt her cheeks flush. "Sorry."

"Don't be. Rachel, I can't thank you enough for what you've done."

"But I haven't done anything."

"You saved Heath's life."

"That's my job."

"I know what happened in there." He put his hand over hers, and she held her breath. "You were amazing."

Rachel didn't know what to do. His simple gesture had stolen her senses, made her want to jump up and run out of the building. As if against her will, her gaze inched up to meet his, and everything got a whole lot worse.

She saw his gratitude, right there in those dark eyes. Fine, great, but there was something more, and it was going to drown her if she didn't look away. Only she didn't. Couldn't. And the connection between them strengthened, blossomed, filled her with a yearning that made her want to cry.

"When you were there, standing by Heath…" Guy began. "I can't explain it. I felt so calm. Just seconds before, I'd been ready to chop off someone's head, kick down the whole building, and then, there you were, and…"

Pulling in a breath, Rachel drew her hand away, surprised she wasn't shaking. She'd worked her entire adult life to keep from feeling like this about someone, especially her boss. Staring intently at her teacup, she cleared her throat. "I'm glad I could be there for you, Guy. I'm so terribly sorry for what you've had to go through."

He had some coffee, shifted in his seat. "Anyway, thank you."

"What are you going to do?"

"Find him."

"How?"

"I don't know. I'll start with the police…see if they can help, although I don't have high hopes. Get on the phone, see if there's anyone at that number."

"At least you know that Heath's in the best possible hands."

He nodded. "If it's Noonan's, we'll have to be on top of it for the rest of his life."

"But there's so much that can be done," Rachel said. "From what I've seen, he just has the pulmonary stenosis, and they're treating that aggressively. I think he's going to be fine."

Guy smiled weakly. She thought she saw his eyes glisten, but it could have been the candlelight.

"What about your ex-wife?" she asked.

"Tammy's coming. I'm not sure when she'll get here, but I'll deal with that when it happens."

"You sound as if you don't want her to come."

His expression turned bitter. "She's not very good with children. Even healthy ones."

"What about Heather?"

"Heather was a mess when I first met her. Wild, rebellious and furious with the world."

"It sounded to me like you two got along pretty well."

"Eventually. It took some doing. I'm ashamed to say that the effort was mostly hers."

"I can't believe that."

He looked at her with a sternness that she recognized well. "Believe it. We used to go out on my boat a lot. It's practically the only time we were together. She loved sailing as much as I did."

"That's wonderful."

"Not really. I never went because Heather wanted to sail. I went for myself, and if she wanted to come along, I didn't stop her. That was about the only time I saw her. I was always at work."

"Your work is important."

"More important than my daughter? My wife? My family?"

"You're being awfully tough on yourself."

"I deserve worse."

"I'm all for self-flagellation. In fact, I've been known to indulge quite often. But now isn't the time. You have things to do, and none of it includes beating yourself to a bloody pulp."

He nodded. "You're right. I just wish I had a plan."

"Okay, then. That's what we'll do. We'll think this through and make a plan."

Rachel could see him physically relax, not just his face but his body. His shoulders eased and even his color changed.

Just then, a waiter came to the table, bringing them dinner. It looked wonderful, and they wasted no time digging in. Her last meal had been a granola bar at her desk hours ago.

"Let's start with Stan," she said as soon as the initial feeding frenzy had calmed. "Why would he lock her up?"

"Because he's a sick bastard who deserves to be in prison?"

"Aside from that."

"I was thinking that very thing," Guy said. He ate a bite of chicken, then put his fork down. "What if it had something to do with Heather's pregnancy."

"What, he wanted to keep her so she couldn't run off with the baby?"

"Well, why didn't he hold her captive before she was pregnant?"

"Maybe he got crazier."

For a few minutes, they ate in silence. Rachel still hadn't shaken the sensations that had swamped her when Guy had touched her hand. She felt confused. What in the hell was going on with her?

She'd never seen Guy like this before; his emotions were so close to the surface it was painful. He'd let down his guard big-time, and laid his heart at her feet.

She didn't want that. On the other hand, she was so drawn to him that it made her dizzy.

If it had been anyone else, she would never have agreed to dinner. In fact, she would have made every excuse in the book to stay as far away as possible.

But she was here, and more than that, she wanted to help. Desperately. Which meant she should back the heck off.

"She mentioned another girl in the diary," Guy said. "The woman before Heather. At first, Heather believed Stan had left his former girlfriend because she was nuts, but then she wrote that the girl had been pregnant, and Stan had left her after the baby was born. When Heather asked him about the baby, he got furious with her and told her never to talk about it again."

"I don't understand," Rachel said.

"I'm not sure I do, either, but maybe it's a pattern. Maybe he's one of those sociopaths who want to own a woman completely, and when he has her truly over a barrel, with his child no less, he loses interest. Moves on to the next victim."

"If that's true, there's probably a string of women out there. Who knows? Maybe he gets these girls pregnant for a reason."

Guy nodded. "I've considered that, too, which means checking on adoption scams. God, what a thought."

"It's too soon to tell, but I don't think you can discount anything at this point," she said.

"So I have a place to begin."

"Which is?"

"An ad in the *L.A. Times*. Homes for unwed mothers. Adoption agencies that the police are checking out."

Rachel put her fork down. "Yes, yes. That's good."

He closed his eyes and rested his fingertips on his lids. "It's a start."

"It's a great start."

He put his hands down and looked at her. "I have no business asking you this, but will you help? Maybe put together an ad for the *L.A. Times*?"

"Of course," she said, then mentally kicked herself.

"Wait, no. Hey, I'm being incredibly selfish, and I don't want to do that anymore. Forget I said a word. You've done so much already. I'm sure my sister can lend a hand."

He must have seen something in her expression when she'd agreed to help him, a flash of reluctance, perhaps. And it made her feel like a first-class heel. "Nonsense. Remember, I've got tomorrow off, so I'll come by and we can work together. After that, I'm on days, and…"

"That would be great." He nodded, as if to himself. "Fantastic."

She finished her tea and folded her napkin across her plate. "It's time for me to get back to work. Miles to go, and all that…"

"Sure, sure." He signaled the waiter for the check while she reached for her purse.

When the bill came Rachel slid out of the booth, cash in hand. "What's my share?" she asked.

"Are you joking? This is on me, and if you say a word, I'll tell everyone at the E.R. I took you out to dinner."

She laughed. "You don't think they know already?"

"True."

As soon as he paid the bill, they walked to the door, Guy touching the small of her back with the warm palm of his hand.

Again, Rachel's whole body went into some kind of hyperawareness. Her breath caught and she had to concentrate on putting one foot in front of the other. She walked a little faster, and his hand fell away. Only then did she breathe calmly again.

It was ridiculous. She tried to think of some way to explain her reaction, or of some other time when she had felt like this, but nothing came to mind. Not even her first kiss. Not even the first time she'd made love.

CALLIE KNEW SHE WAS calling late, and that Max Zirinsky had probably gone home long ago, but she had the police chief's office number in her PalmPilot, and she didn't have a phone book handy.

The cell rang twice. "Courage Bay Police Department."

"Chief Zirinsky, please."

"One moment."

She listened to a snippet of "Moon River," then a deep, masculine voice said, "Zirinsky."

"Chief. This is Callie Baker."

There was a slight pause. "What can I do for you, Callie?"

"I wanted to know if you'd ever heard of a man named Bruce Nepom."

"I've heard the name. Why?"

Callie could easily picture Max. Although their paths only crossed professionally now, at one point they had almost been family. Max was a cousin of Callie's ex-husband.

"He died this morning," Callie told him. "Crushed by his roof during the storm."

Max gave her an address, and she opened Nepom's file to verify they were talking about the same man.

"That's right."

"I see," Max said. "What about him?"

"There were some anomalies—particularly a deep concussion in the back of the skull that doesn't fit the profile of a crush injury."

"You think there's more to it than a weather-related accident?"

"I don't have anything concrete, but I thought you might like to be at the autopsy."

"When is it scheduled?"

"Day after tomorrow, at ten-thirty."

"I'll be there. And Callie, if you don't mind, could I get the doctor's report on the initial injury?"

"Of course. I'll have it there for you."

"Thank you," he said.

Their business was over, but Callie was reluctant to hang up. "I imagine it's been a nightmare day for you."

"You got that right. The traffic problems alone would have kept us busy, but there was an incredible amount of damage. It's going to be a while until we get a handle on it."

"Today we had a lot of repair injuries."

"Sure, that makes sense. I'm surprised there weren't a lot more serious problems."

She picked up her cooled cup of coffee and took a sip. "We had a lot of traffic in the E.R., but not much that was deadly, thank goodness."

"I wish I could say the same for this damn city."

"You've had a lot on your plate lately."

She heard his sigh across the line. "Too much, Callie. There's been way the hell too much death around Courage Bay, and I'll be damned if I'll let it continue."

CHAPTER SIX

THE LIGHTS WERE DIMMED, the soft padding of the nurses' feet faded into the background along with the beeping of the heart monitors and hush of respirators. Guy had never felt more helpless. Or more determined.

He cradled Heath in his arms, thinking about what this little one had to face. If he got through the first few weeks of his infancy, he'd still have developmental difficulties, physical and mental. But that didn't mean he wouldn't have a meaningful life.

Guy had seen many patients over the years who had given birth to developmentally challenged children, and while not ignoring the shock and the disappointment these parents faced, he'd made it a point to let them know that their children would be a gift to their lives. There were two support groups his team had helped put together in Courage Bay to help families cope and thrive in such situations. His experience was that parents who had the right attitude really did find that their special children made their lives rich and blessed. There were significant hurdles to conquer, but that created a bond that was unique in all the world.

It shocked him to realize that while he'd believed

that intellectually, he hadn't truly understood it until now.

The protectiveness he felt toward this child eclipsed any emotion he could ever remember feeling. It was stronger than his love of medicine, stronger than his feelings for Tammy, even in the beginning. It was new, and frightening. Within less than twenty-four hours, his priorities had completely shifted.

He had to save this boy's life. He had to find Heath's father, and make sure that bastard paid for what he'd done to Heather and her baby.

It occurred to him that before he'd known about Heath, the highlight of his week was knowing his boat had been safe from the storm. Now the boat seemed a trifle, an extravagance with no meaning.

No meaning.

It all came down to that, didn't it? What had it all meant? The success of his career? The pursuit of winning, of money, of women—trophies to impress himself. And in the process, he'd turned a blind eye to those who needed him, to those who could have given his life depth. Even his sister and brother, who had offered him family and friendship and continuity, were sidebars to his life. When was the last time he'd really talked to either of them? Not about the hospital, but about their lives? It was as if they'd all agreed that nothing of substance would interfere with the casual day-to-day exchanges, or even holiday gatherings.

He wondered if they had a deeper relationship with each other, or were they as superficial as he was?

He wished Rachel were here, which was just one

more surreal aspect to the day. Why her? Why now? Why did he feel so safe when she was near and want so badly to talk to her in a way he'd never dreamed of before? What the hell was going on with him?

If someone had told him yesterday what he'd be thinking about right now, he would have laughed out loud. Then sent the person to the psych ward.

Heath blew a little bubble between his lips and stirred slightly. All notions of craziness fled as a feeling of pure joy cascaded through Guy's body. Heath had moved so little, had responded so faintly, that this was something to celebrate.

He tried to remember the last time he'd prayed. Maybe he never had. But he did now.

THE ELEVATOR TO THE fourth floor was crowded, and Rachel stood in the front, as close to the door as possible. She hadn't found Guy in the E.R. or in his office, although Connie had told her he was doing better today, that he'd just needed some sleep. Rachel had, too.

After her shift had ended that morning, she'd gone straight home and climbed into bed. One of the first things she'd done when she'd bought her house was to install blackout curtains in her bedroom. Even when it was noon, she was wrapped in cool darkness. She'd also purchased the best sheets she could find, six-hundred-count Egyptian cotton, because bed was huge in her life. Medical school had taught her the importance of taking any and all opportunities to sleep, and she'd nurtured the habit by making her bedroom as cozy and nestlike as possible.

Except this morning, her thoughts had kept her from immediately conking out. For a change, it wasn't one of her patients spinning in her head, it was Guy.

She was still stymied over her reaction to him. She'd known him for two years, and nothing like this had happened before.

She'd thought he was attractive since day one, no question about that, but when he'd touched her last night it was like being zapped by a live wire. Why? He'd touched her before. A hand on her shoulder, a brush of his arm, and while she'd been aware, she hadn't felt—

The first thing that came to mind was awakened. Turned on. In all senses of the phrase. Her focus had shifted, and her awareness had gone from fuzzy to startlingly sharp.

It made no sense. If she'd been diagnosing someone in her condition, she would have laughed and told them it was nothing life threatening. A simple case of lust.

Lust?

That was absurd.

Not that Rachel was immune, but it hadn't happened to her in a long, long time.

And why in hell would she feel lust for a man in so much pain? God, maybe she was a sicko, some kind of sadist.

Well, if that were true, it was the first she'd been aware of it.

Come to think of it, it wasn't his grief that had made her see him differently, it was his raw humanity. He'd unmasked himself yesterday, and for the first time, she'd seen the man behind the white coat.

Okay, so she wasn't a pervert, which was good. But she was deeply affected by Guy Giroux, which was bad. Very bad.

The elevator stopped and she got out, heading directly to the NICU. It felt odd to be here in her civvies. She'd worn jeans, a maroon turtleneck and leather jacket—a typical choice for days off. But it felt too casual for the hospital.

Guy, as she'd suspected, was with Heath, but he wasn't alone. The whole team was there, standing around the incubator, deep in discussion. She thought about joining them, but decided it wasn't her place. Instead she went to the nurses' station and asked for a piece of notepaper. Quickly she told Guy she'd been by, but that she didn't want to interrupt. If he needed her, she was on her cell. She signed the message Rachel and noted the time.

After folding the paper, she asked the nurse to give it to Guy when he was finished with the consult.

Then she quickly left the NICU and the hospital and headed toward her car.

The January afternoon had a slight chill, and Rachel shivered, but she didn't start the engine once she was inside her car. Instead, she looked past the parking lot to the grass and the trees. The hospital was beautifully landscaped, and though the storm had shaken things up, everything around her seemed reborn, and refreshingly lush.

Rachel wondered what the beach would look like. Probably rough and wild and beautiful.

She started the car. It was one of her few indulgences. For the most part, she was careful with her money, making sure her portfolio was diversified and safe. But certain things, like her sheets, the occasional cashmere sweater and her Mustang, were luxuries she allowed herself. The car was a reminder of her father. They hadn't shared a lot, but he'd let her help when he tinkered with his cars.

And now she had one of her own. She loved this baby, and she did most of the maintenance herself. There were definitely some advantages to having no social life.

She headed toward Courage Bay's main shopping district, although there was nothing she had to look for there. Then she noticed a nail salon, walk-ins welcome. She glanced at her fingers. Ugh. The nails were short by necessity, but they didn't have to be so ugly.

She found a parking space and decided right then and there to have both a manicure and pedicure. She needed to indulge herself. Relax. And try not to think about Guy.

GUY GOT THE NOTE from Rachel at four-fifteen. The day had disappeared in consultations, lab reports and phone calls.

It was the phone calls he wanted to discuss with Rachel, but not yet. He needed to get home, shower, change clothes. He didn't want to leave Heath, even though he trusted his colleagues to watch him through the night. But if he wasn't rested, he wouldn't be able to find Stan, let alone handle his responsibilities at the hospital.

As he drove, he thanked God for his team. Connie had

made sure he was covered, and Callie Baker had stopped in to see him this afternoon to let him know she was there for him if he needed her, and that the entire hospital staff was at his disposal. Everyone was in full support mode for his revised staffing schedule, which was yet another shocker in a considerable stack of them. No one had complained about the double shifts, the loss of weekends off. That kind of support was hard to accept.

He paid attention to the road while he planned his evening. City road crews were still cleaning up from the storm, and several lights were out at major intersections. In the little shopping district near his home, Sam's Hardware was boarded up, as was the dry cleaners. The storm seemed a lifetime ago, especially when the sky was clear and the air so clean. His personal storm wasn't clearing up so handily.

But no thinking. Not yet. Get home. Power nap. Shower. Rachel.

He turned onto Druid Lane, past Mrs. Allen's house. Three cars were parked out front, one with the logo of an insurance company marked on the side. Glad she was taken care of, and that there would be no yapping dogs tonight, Guy pressed the button for his garage and slid the SUV next to his Corvette.

Everything ached as he walked into the house, and he decided to shower first, power nap second. Everything else would follow in its own good time.

No. Actually, there was something that had to be done right now. He picked up the phone and dialed Rachel's cell. He got her voice mail. "Rachel, if you're not busy, come over tonight. I'll fix some dinner. Around seven, okay? I want to talk to you about Stan and that whole business. Anyway, come if you can. If not, no sweat."

RACHEL RANG GUY'S DOORBELL and suddenly felt like a moron for bringing wine. This wasn't really a social call. Did she have time to run back to her car and put it in the trunk? No, he'd ask what she was doing, and she couldn't think that fast. When the lock clicked, she panicked and tossed the bottle in the big hedge. Only, it didn't disappear. It just bounced once and sat there on the green branches, red bow and all.

"Rachel."

She turned to the door, slapping a grin on her face and trying desperately for an air of nonchalance. "Guy."

He looked a bit puzzled, glanced behind her, then stepped back. "Come on in."

She walked in, passing him on his left so he wouldn't look outside and bust her cold.

"Thank you," he said.

"You need to stop that," she chided. "There's no reason to thank me. I'm sure you'd do the same for me."

He walked behind her and put his hands on her collar, but he didn't remove her jacket. Instead, he leaned softly forward. She thought she heard him take a deep breath, then he said, "You'd be wrong."

She shivered as he slowly pulled her jacket off, touching her upper arms briefly. Not good. She'd just gotten here, and she'd made a fool of herself twice. No more shivering allowed. This was not really personal. He needed a sounding board, nothing more. And she was the one who'd opened her big mouth last night and said she'd help.

Guy cleared his throat, then hung her coat in the closet. Rachel took the opportunity to look around. She'd never been here before. When Guy hosted social events for the staff, they were inevitably held at the Bar and Grill. His place was beautiful, lots of white marble, modern paintings, elegant furniture. But it was a bit cold, as if a decorator had had her way when Guy was at work. "Nice," she said.

He waved away the compliment. "I hope you don't mind salmon again so soon," he said.

"Mind? I love it."

"Great. Come with me," he said, taking her hand and leading her past a large great room that was much the same as the foyer and into a kitchen where everything changed.

"Oh, Guy," she exclaimed.

"My other passion," he told her. "Aside from sailing."

She worked her way around the huge room slowly, examining the big wraparound counter made of smooth granite, the six-burner professional stove, two ovens, two microwaves, the subzero freezer and fridge. She ran her hand over the deep double sink with the grocer's spigot, and checked out the cubbyholes built into the shelves to hold baking equipment. In the center of the kitchen stood an island with oversize drawers, a separate sink and butcher-block cutting board. It was the most perfect kitchen she'd ever seen. "This is amazing."

He smiled like a proud papa. "It's criminal that I use it so infrequently."

"You must quit your job tonight and become a full-time chef."

He laughed out loud, and she blushed when she realized what she'd said.

"God, I needed that," he said. "Laughter. It really does heal, doesn't it."

She nodded, remembering what he'd been through and what he was facing. "Tell me about Heath."

"Wine, then talk."

"Hold on." She held up her hand. "I forgot the wine in my car."

"Great. You need your jacket."

"I'll just be gone a second."

"I'll get busy at my new career."

She grinned all the way outside, then stood by the hedge, getting chilled in the cool night air, for what she thought was an appropriate time to get to her car and back. When she finally went into the house, she felt as if she was visiting a friend. Wow. She hadn't done that in a long time. Her best and pretty much only friend, Allie, lived in San Francisco.

As she passed the great room, she could hear Guy puttering. Maybe that's what all this was about. She needed a friend. Someone she could talk to. She could have a boss for a friend, right? Who cared if he was male. Men could be friends.

As she turned the corner of the kitchen and saw him standing at the counter chopping herbs, Rachel knew immediately that while Guy might indeed become a friend, that wasn't at all what she really wanted from him. Not by a long shot.

CHAPTER SEVEN

GUY LOOKED UP when he heard Rachel approach. He scarcely noticed the bottle of wine in her hand, caught as he was by the tension barely concealed in her face, in her whole body. He put down his knife, trying like hell not to panic. "What's wrong? Is it Heath?"

She blinked. "What?"

"Did you hear something?" He walked around the island. "Was it a phone call?"

"No, no." She held up the bottle. "I just got this."

He let the information sink in. Whatever had changed her mood, it wasn't about the boy. "Is something else bothering you?"

She smiled, although he wasn't completely convinced. "Yeah, I'm hungry."

"That's something I can fix. Why don't you pour the wine, and I'll finish the fish." He grabbed the corkscrew and handed it to her, his fingers brushing the side of her hand. She was cold, but he had the feeling it wasn't just from the air outside.

She'd only been gone a few minutes. When she'd walked out of the kitchen, she'd seemed relaxed. So what had she thought of, walking to her car? That she shouldn't be having dinner with her boss? Could she see how much he wanted her here, and had that made her want to get the hell away from him?

The cork popped as he turned to the stove. The salmon was already seasoned and he was heating the cast-iron pan. Once it was hot enough, he put the two fillets in it, the sizzle loud in the still house.

Rachel poured the wine as he went to the other side of the kitchen, where a CD player had been built into the cabinet. A live concert by Jean-Pierre Rampal seemed perfect, the lilting flute lightening the mood. Then he got his glass and held it up for a toast. "To moments of respite," he said.

She smiled again, and although there was more heart in it this time, he knew beyond a doubt that something had changed, and not for the better.

They both took a sip of wine, and while Rachel stared somewhere off to his right, Guy noticed that her lips had left just a trace of pale pink lipstick on the edge of the glass. Interesting. Rachel always wore red lipstick at work. He'd never given it much thought, except for the perfectly natural observation that anyone who didn't want to kiss her when they saw it was insane. But here, on her day off, she wore a much lighter tint, softer.

"So what else can I do?" she asked, putting her glass down.

He looked at the table in the dining room. Everything was set up, ready for the meal. "You can light the candles," he said. "And toss the salad."

While she went to complete her first task, he finished up the dressing for the Tuscan-bread salad. By the time she was back in the kitchen, it was finished, and he had to turn over the salmon.

He wondered if he should say something. Ask her what happened. Or maybe the right thing to do was to let her off the hook. Give her an excuse to bail as soon as dinner was over. He'd stepped outside the line yesterday and taken her with him, and truthfully, he had no right to do that. The woman had offered him simple human comfort and consolation, and he'd taken advantage of her. Not terribly surprising, considering his record.

Maybe this was a trip he had to take on his own. That he'd wanted a beautiful woman to ease his pain wasn't a stretch. He'd always gone for what was easiest, safest, coziest for himself.

But not this time. He wasn't willing to lose Rachel in the E.R. She was the kind of doctor the hospital needed, and if he got involved with her, it would inevitably end in disaster. For her, at least.

So this time, he'd give it a break. He'd planned to ask Rachel for help in finding Stan, but he could hire a private detective. As for Heath, Guy had access to a world of medical experts. Rachel was a luxury, and off-limits.

He finished reducing the glaze just as the salmon completed cooking. Then he checked on the pot of orzo, which was perfect. He added spices, spooned it into a dish, then took that and the salad to the table.

"Come sit," he said. "Serve us salads. I'll be right back with the salmon."

She took her glass and went to her seat. He got the rest of the dinner and brought it with him, then sat down across from her.

"This smells fantastic," she said.

"I hope it tastes even better."

She smiled, took a bite of the salad. Her eyes widened. "Oh, my."

He grinned as he arranged the main course on two plates. "Another bonus to cooking. Immediate gratification."

"I'll say."

He settled back in his seat, watching her as he sipped the wine. "I'm pretty good at that."

"I know. This salad is unbelievable."

"No, I mean the immediate-gratification part."

"Ah."

He was hungry, but for the moment, he didn't pick up his fork. "Why did you go into medicine?"

"When I was a teenager, I had a friend who got sick. I spent a lot of time at the hospital, and all I wanted to do was help."

He nodded. "Sounds like you found your calling."

"I'm lucky."

"You went to UCLA?"

"And Baylor. And I'll confess, it wasn't easy. My roommates hardly studied, and I was constantly hitting the books. I had to read everything twice. God, it was a nightmare."

"I was like your roommates. It wasn't difficult for me."

She arched her eyebrow. "Way to make friends, Dr. Giroux."

"I didn't say that to make you feel bad. It was just an observation. Most things in my life came easily. Although I'm beginning to think it wasn't such a gift."

"Are you kidding? I would have killed to get through school like that."

"But you did this incredibly difficult thing, slugged it out the whole way, and now you know."

"Know what?"

"That you can do it. That you have what it takes to do the hard stuff."

She looked at her wine. "I suppose so."

Guy leaned forward, putting both elbows on the table. "We—my family—were all about medicine. Getting into med school, making sure we lived up to my father's reputation."

"Those were big shoes to fill. Everyone knows about Paul Giroux."

"Yeah. He was a great doctor."

"But?"

"Not such a great father."

"He had a lot on his plate."

"Yeah, and the three of us were a side dish."

"You and I both know how hard it is to do what we do and have a family. There aren't enough hours in the day. Not enough energy to go around."

"True. It's a bitch. Although I've seen people do it."

She moved her salad plate to the right and tasted the salmon. Her appreciative noises made him grin. Then she became serious again. "Something has to give, Guy. You can't be all things to all people. Either you're a great trauma doctor, or you're a great father. Not both."

"Why not?"

"It doesn't work that way. Who do you know that has it all?"

"Emmett Rosen."

"Emmett Rosen is a consulting surgeon. He doesn't work full-time."

"But he's a great doctor."

"Part-time."

"He's a great father."

"That's what he chose. His family is his priority. But he couldn't do your job and have the same quality of life at home."

Guy stabbed his salad. "I suppose."

Rachel looked at him. "You aren't responsible for Heather's death."

"Whoa. Big leap there, isn't it?"

"I know you're beating yourself up for not knowing that Heather was pregnant. That she was caught up in a dangerous situation. But what you're forgetting is that while you were living together, you made a difference in her life. You know you did. Maybe if you'd been her real father—"

"I was as real as it gets. At least for a while. And you know how I made a difference? I wasn't mean. I took her out on the boat. When it was convenient, I listened to her. When it wasn't, I walked away without a backward glance. She was grateful to me because her real parents were, if it's at all possible, even more self-obsessed than I was. It wasn't love she had, it was leftovers. Table scraps."

"Guy, stop it. Right now. You may not have been "Father Knows Best," but you did what you could. And it mattered to Heather."

He ate, hardly tasting the food. This was torture, and

he hated it. What had happened to the life he'd so carefully built for himself? Everything had been running smoothly. He had his E.R. and the house he loved. When he had time, he had the boat. And then there were the women. So beautiful, so eager. Wanting to please him in every way, and he lapped it up. When they got too close, when they wanted something back, he walked. Bailed. Congratulating himself the whole time that he'd never lied to any of them. He'd told them up front that he wasn't looking for a serious relationship, then proceeded to milk them dry.

And he hadn't cared. That was the beauty of it. He hadn't given one damn about the consequences. He'd figured they were grown women, and as long as he didn't lie, everything was copacetic.

He wanted that life back. He let go of his fork and pushed his plate away. "Damn it, I did not ask for this."

Rachel sat up straighter. "I know. But Heather went to the only place she could. She wanted to be safe, to save her child, so she came to you."

"That's not what I'm talking about."

"I don't understand."

He stood up and looked at her plate. She wasn't half finished, so he couldn't just ask her to leave. He had to calm the hell down. "It doesn't matter. Go ahead and eat. I'm just going to get the wine." He went into the kitchen so she couldn't see him. Then he closed his eyes, willed the past two days to go away.

But they wouldn't go away. Heath was still on the fourth floor. The child had no one else but Guy. For now, at least.

He opened his eyes. Tammy was on her way. The thought made him instantly feel better. Tammy was Heath's real grandmother. The boy was her responsibility, not Guy's. That didn't mean he'd just walk away. Guy intended to find that bastard Stan and make sure he paid. But in the end, Heath was not Guy's concern. When the baby was well enough to go home, it would be to Europe. To Tammy's. And Guy's life could go right back to normal.

He grabbed the wine bottle and took the pie out of the fridge to let it get to room temperature. When he went back to the table, he felt one hell of a lot better. "So," he said, "you like sailing?"

Rachel blinked at him. Her pretty little mouth opened just enough for him to get a glimpse of the tops of her even, white teeth. "Pardon?"

"Sailing." He topped off her glass, then his own. As soon as he sat down, he dug into his food as if he hadn't eaten for weeks.

"Yes, I like sailing, I suppose."

He swallowed. "Then you haven't really been sailing. It's the most incredible… When the wind fills the sails, flying over the water. It's—"

"Amazing."

"Right."

"Okay," she said. "What just happened?"

Guy laughed. "Stress, my friend. Or the release thereof. I'm sorry. I've been a real needy pain in the ass, and I promise, that's over. Look, after this, I've got a killer dessert. I promise you'll love it. And then we can go back to our lives, okay? Just the way things used to be."

"Sounds great," she said. "Totally unrealistic, but great."

"Ah, now, why are we bursting bubbles?"

She hesitated, then met his gaze. "Heath."

He nodded slowly. "Heath."

"That little guy is still in a lot of trouble."

"True. And I'm going to do everything in my power to make him well."

"That's going to take a great deal."

"I know." The tension was coming back. And deeper than that, the fear. God, the fear. "I know," he said again, giving up dinner as a lost cause. He stood up, unable to sit in his chair another second. "What he needs is a mother, but he doesn't have one."

"He's got you, and—"

"And his grandmother? Look, the woman is a beauty, I'll give her that. But as I told you, she never won any mother-of-the-year awards. Heather was a healthy, alert child. She had to be. She had to take care of herself. As for her father, shit. He was so busy going from one harebrained scheme to another, it's amazing he even remembered he had a daughter."

"Right now, what Heath needs is someone to care for him. I can't think of anyone on earth who could do a better job. That's it. That's all you have to do. Don't look ahead to tomorrow. It'll come no matter what, and if you're not a hundred percent on task today, Heath loses."

He was going to say something, but he didn't. Instead, he simply looked at the woman sitting at his table. She was really something, especially right at this moment. Strong, in charge. She would have been a great general, a terrific ship captain. Instead, she was his colleague, which was great, but he wanted more. How much more, he wasn't sure. Just...more.

"What?" she asked. "Is it so hard to do that?"

"No. You're right. Whatever happens with Tammy, I'll deal with it. The only thing I can afford to think about is Heath. Which is why I need you to help me."

"Uh, Guy—"

"Hear me out, okay? All I'm asking is that you make a few phone calls." He sat down in the chair, next to her. "I know this guy. He's a lieutenant in the LAPD. Maybe he knows something about Stan, about this possible scam he might running." He put his hand on her arm, feeling much more than warmth where his palm met her sweater. "And you mentioned homes for unwed mothers. Jeez, I don't even know if they have those anymore, but you could call around. I know, it's a lot to ask, and you have your hands full in the E.R.—"

She put up her free hand, stopping him. "Wait."

He sat back, breaking the connection between them—at least the physical one. He hoped there was still something else going on between them on another level.

"I'll do what I can, okay? Let's have some coffee. Fill me in on this policeman you know, and I'll call him tomorrow. I'll follow up on the pregnant-women thing, too. All you have to worry about is Heath."

Guy sighed. "Great. That's so great."

Rachel got up, but not before he saw a flush brighten her cheeks. She faced him, her expression calm and professional. "It's about friendship."

"Right. Friendship."

"Why don't you get the coffee ready while I check out your bathroom."

He laughed. "It's down that hall, to your left," he said, pointing past the living room.

"Thanks."

Guy watched her as she walked away. He liked the way she held herself, so tall and straight. And the way her smooth, glossy hair swung down almost to the small of her back. He wished it wasn't in a ponytail, though. He'd like to see her hair free, loose. He'd like to see Rachel the same way.

Carefree, abandoned, wild. Lying underneath him, naked, in his bed. The images came tumbling, one after another, and like a randy kid, he felt himself harden. "Oh, shit," he whispered. What the hell had just happened? Not five minutes ago, he'd decided to stop crossing the line. To let Rachel get back to her rightful place in his life.

His good intentions had gone to hell, along with everything else. Guy stood up, wanting very much to punch something. Heading into the kitchen, he pushed the button on the coffeemaker. As the brewing started, he put his hands on the granite counter and stared at nothing at all. "What the hell's happening to me?" he said out loud.

No one answered. All he was left with was the knowledge that he could take only one tiny step at a time, and try like hell not to make too big an ass of himself. It wasn't going to be easy.

CHAPTER EIGHT

RACHEL RAN HER HAND over the pink marble counter-top in Guy's bathroom. It was a beautiful room, well appointed with elegant sconces, brass hardware and a unique pale stone floor. But it had a different feel from the kitchen. That felt like Guy's room, as if he'd really put himself into the space. The bathroom was more of a decorator's dream, and it reminded Rachel of her own home.

She remembered the line she'd read from Heather's diary, that she wanted so much to decorate a house. Rachel hadn't had the time or the patience to do any decorating. She'd hired a woman from a local interior design firm and pretty much left her to it. And Rachel had gotten what she'd paid for. Everything was perfectly coordinated, even the artwork. But it wasn't Rachel.

She had to laugh at that. She had no idea what she would have done if she'd been faced with the task alone. Style? Her clothing was more utilitarian than stylish, and her hair was about as simple as it could get. Even her makeup served her purposes—to make her look professional, in charge.

Other priorities crowded her life, and yet every once

in a while, she regretted not being able to do the things other women found time to do.

But that was hardly important now. She'd agreed to help Guy, despite her reservations, and what she had to do now was swing their conversation into the concrete. Ask him about the police lieutenant, find out exactly what Guy wanted her to do.

Rachel left the bathroom and headed back to the kitchen. Guy was in the living room, however, and on the coffee table he'd placed a tray with a carafe of coffee, two cups, all the accoutrements, and a large bottle of Courvoisier XO Imperial next to a delicious-looking cream pie.

"How do you like your coffee?" he asked, ushering her to the leather club chair beside the couch. "I'm hoping you'll try a little of the cognac. It's considered to be one of the best in the world."

"I don't know if I should."

"Tell you what. You fix your own coffee and I'll go get the snifters."

She busied herself doing just that, and was settled in her chair when Guy came back holding the glasses.

"May I tempt you?"

"A little, but that's all."

He honored her wishes, pouring a bit into the curved bowl of the snifter. The liquor was dark and rich, and it reminded Rachel of the color of Guy's eyes. When he handed her the glass, he hesitated, meeting her gaze. His smile came slowly, as if he'd seen something that surprised him. Delighted him.

She felt her cheeks heat and turned away to look at

the stone fireplace that was the centerpiece of the room. "Did you live here with Tammy?"

He sat down on the couch, sipped the cognac and closed his eyes for a second. When he opened them, he looked right at her. "I bought this house for her. She didn't want to move to Courage Bay, so I had to make the package sweet."

"Why didn't she want to move here?"

He nodded. "We met in Los Angeles. That's where she lived—had lived her whole life. I was teaching at your alma mater, working on trauma protocols. She was a guest at a friend's party. We hit it off."

"I see."

"God, she was something back then. A little thing, no bigger than a minute, but she lit up a room. I couldn't take my eyes off her."

"How long after you met did you get married?"

"Five months."

"Wow."

"Yeah." He leaned back on the couch pillows and put his feet on the coffee table. "In retrospect, it wasn't the brightest thing I've ever done."

"So you moved Tammy and Heather up here?"

"After a fight, yes. She had friends in Los Angeles. She fancied herself a painter."

"Well, if she was into that—"

"Actually, she wasn't. She did, however, like to buy supplies, hang out with artists, talk about art. Only she never actually finished anything. Not in all the time I knew her."

"And how was it once you got here?"

"She found the art community here. Decorated this house. Had an affair with one of the nude models that posed for her in class."

"Ouch."

"Yeah. To say Tammy and I weren't good for each other would be an understatement."

"I'm sorry."

"I was sorry, too. Sorry for myself. But the truth was, Dr. Browne, she was acting out of self-defense. I was a rotten husband. I moved her away from everything she knew and loved, and then I left her to fend for herself. I figured if I let her spend my money, she'd be fine. That's not how it worked out."

"Guy—"

"Yeah, yeah." He sipped some Courvoisier, waving his hand in her direction. "No more of this blasted personal talk. I promise."

"You said something about a police lieutenant?"

"Right. Richie Montgomery. Good ol' boy from Natchez, Mississippi, transplanted to Los Angeles in the early 1970s. Hell of a sailor."

"What do you want me to tell him?"

He closed one eye, studying her with the other. "I have no business asking you to do this, but screw it, I'm asking anyway. I'd like you to read Heather's diary— all of it. Then talk to Richie, give him whatever information you think would help him put together a picture of the guy. Fax him relevant pages. See if he knows anything about where young, pregnant women strung out on drugs would go."

He closed his eyes again. "I'd do it myself, but I

want every spare second to be with Heath tomorrow. Once you get something concrete, then we'll reconnoiter. Figure out what to do next."

"Would you prefer me to concentrate on Heath?"

"It probably would be better, but I need to do that."

She nodded. "Of course."

"Thank you," he said very softly. Then he rested the snifter on his chest, his eyes still closed.

Rachel looked at him. He seemed relaxed, comfortable now, even though she knew he was filled with guilt and worry. Her gaze moved from his boot-clad feet up his long legs and well-worn jeans. He'd rolled up the sleeves of his pale yellow oxford shirt, and his arms were dusted with dark hair, although the sinews and muscles were clearly defined. His hands, remarkable, strong hands, had been a source of fascination for a long time. So large, and yet able to do the most delicate work. He was an artist with a suture, gifted beyond belief with a scalpel. Even at rest, his fingers seemed capable and sure, as if a person's life would be safe within their grasp.

Then she reached his profile, and suddenly a drink seemed a very wise thing. The cognac melted with a velvet fire down her throat, warming her all the way to her toes. She doubted she'd seen a more handsome face than Guy Giroux's. His dark, bushy eyebrows made him look very serious, at least when he wanted to. But when he smiled, all seriousness disappeared, and it was almost impossible not to grin along with him. That's because his eyes, so smoky and dark, had an inner light that made his face shine with his good humor. It didn't hurt that his smile was equally mesmerizing.

Altogether, he was one of those men who had women panting after him, but the odd thing was, he wasn't a total ass about it. Rachel had never once seen him act in anything but a professional manner. Although there had been times she'd been embarrassed at the behavior of the women around him.

It wasn't really fair that he was so bright and had those good looks. Not that he was perfect. She'd heard too many tales of heartbreak from too many women to believe that. Which was why it was so much easier just to think of him as her boss. His personal life wasn't something she cared to know about. Not just because it was so…enthusiastically lived, but because she hadn't escaped the pull of the man. Just like the nurses, the secretaries, the other female doctors, Rachel was drawn to the blatant sexuality of the man.

What had she gotten herself into? She'd just agreed to work with him on a strictly personal basis. Diving into his life…right into the deep end. Great. Just peachy.

She put her glass on the coffee table, next to her untouched coffee, expecting him to react. He didn't. When she stood and walked over to the couch, she saw why. He was asleep, his brandy snifter perfectly balanced on his chest.

She thought about waking him, but the poor man had been through so much today. Instead, she inched the glass from between his fingers, then took the cashmere throw from the other end of the couch and draped it over his lower body.

He hadn't moved an inch. His lips were slightly

parted, and the worry that had marred his face since yesterday had disappeared, leaving him sweetly peaceful.

She leaned down, not touching him at all, except where her lips brushed his forehead. His skin was cool, smooth. And yet it warmed her in a way she didn't want to acknowledge.

As soon as she'd retrieved her purse and jacket, Rachel slipped out of his house, away from his spell.

Her decision was made. She'd agreed to help Guy. She'd make the phone calls and do whatever else he asked to find Heath's father. But she'd stop all this other nonsense, stat.

GUY WOKE WITH A START as his feet slipped off the coffee table. He looked across at the club chair, but Rachel wasn't in it. Then he checked his watch. It was after three. Great. He'd fallen asleep right in front of her.

His neck and back were stiff, so he stood up and stretched. Bed beckoned and he headed toward the back of the house, unbuttoning his shirt as he walked.

He still wasn't sure if the dinner had been a mistake. Rachel had been great, but she hadn't been able to disguise her discomfort completely. It still mystified him that he'd pulled her into his drama, that her presence seemed so necessary.

Was it because she'd been the doctor to deliver Heath? Rachel had been with Heather in her last moments. Would Guy have felt the same if it had been one of the male attendings?

No, he was sure he wouldn't.

He walked past his bed into the dressing room, where

he tossed his shirt into the hamper, then took off the rest of his clothes. Yearning for sleep, he remembered the time and decided to shower now, instead of when he woke up, which would be in a few hours.

Grabbing the sweats and T-shirt he liked to sleep in, he went into the master bath and turned on the water. He loved his shower. It was huge, with dual shower-heads and killer water pressure. As soon as the water was the perfect temperature, he stepped in, letting the heat and steam permeate his senses.

As he relaxed, his thoughts turned back to Rachel. He was embarrassed at how much he'd told her. Shit. None of it was very flattering, either. Whatever hopes he'd once had for being more than colleagues were pretty much down the drain now. If he were honest, he'd known his chances with her were slim to none. Rachel had made that perfectly clear. But it didn't mean he couldn't think about her. Imagine her.

He ran the soap down his chest as the cinema in his mind created vivid pictures of her, none of them in a professional context. Of course, he had to imagine the parts of her he hadn't seen, but that wasn't difficult.

Ah, but to see the real thing, to touch that luminous skin. She was forbidden fruit, which made her even more enticing. A small part of him felt guilt at his las-civious thoughts, but as his imagination went wild, those pangs washed away.

He wallowed in the physical sensations, letting the rest of the world go. Sailing on the waves of lust and desire, he felt free.

At the moment of climax, he gasped her name, keep-

ing his eyes closed until a languorous exhaustion settled over him. He finished washing, all the while curs-
ing the fact that his dreams of Rachel would never
become reality. Still, he had to be grateful for what he
could get. Grateful she hadn't told him to keep his life
to himself.

IT WAS SIX-THIRTY, a time when Rachel was more accus-
tomed to going to sleep than preparing for work. The
beginning of the day shift was always the hardest, when
her circadian rhythms were most fierce in their objec-
tions to the rude change of pace. It didn't help at all that
she'd had a lousy night.

After she'd crawled between her sheets, her mind had
raced with thoughts of Guy. Not about his search for Stan
or his concern for Heath, but simply the man himself.

Everything about him appealed to her. His honesty,
the way he cared about Heath—hell, his willingness to
face his mistakes.

What would she find if she focused the magnifying
glass on herself? A career she loved, that's for sure. An
all-consuming career. Everything else drifted outside
that locus. Her friendship with Allie was an exception,
but how much attention had she paid that relationship?

Allie had been her roommate as an undergraduate.
They'd meshed beautifully, despite the fact that Allie
barely cracked a book and Rachel was forever studying.
It took some work to get over her jealousy, but in the
end it was Allie's uncomplicated friendship that had
won out. That was back when Rachel had a sense of
humor, when they'd go to Monty Python movie mara-

thons and hang out at the Comedy Store until they were practically incoherent with laughter.

Allie had been a breath of fresh air. Totally tone deaf, she'd grown up in a family of musicians. Her mother was first-chair violin at the Pasadena Civic Orchestra, and her father first bassoon. Even her little brother, Randy, was an outstanding guitar player who was a huge success as a recording session player. Poor Allie hadn't fit in at all, but it hadn't diminished her spirit. She was plucky and funny and she charmed everyone in speaking distance.

Even though she wasn't the prettiest girl in the dorm, she was never without a date. Guys and girls wanted to hang out with Allie, and it was Rachel who ended up chasing them out of the room the two of them shared. She'd explained that she had to study, but there was also a part of her that felt hopelessly out of her league when it came to boys and sex and hormones.

Allie used to tell Rachel she needed to loosen up, to let her feelings take the lead for once in her life. But that wasn't Rachel's way.

It hadn't been the way in the Browne family. Her father had been a military man, and that had colored everything in her life. Discipline and order were all that mattered. Second chances were not allowed. There was no room at all for emotion. In the early years though, especially when she'd hit puberty, Rachel had been emotionally hypersensitive. Everything had mattered. Her poor parents had been terrified, and Rachel was left feeling overwhelmed, exhausted, and just plain wrong.

She'd cried all the time. Over a hurt kitten, a slight at school, a B on her report card. Molly's illness and death had taken her to the brink of a nervous breakdown, and at fifteen, Rachel had been prescribed sedatives.

If only she'd found her way to some kind of balance, but that hadn't happened. If she let down the protective walls, everything bombarded her from giddiness to crippling depression. She simply couldn't handle her own emotions, and there wasn't a damn thing she could do about it except guard against situations that left her emotionally vulnerable.

It wasn't the best arrangement, but it was all she had. So why was she even contemplating caring for Guy Giroux? Was she nuts? Aside from all the obvious stuff, the man was going through something intensely personal and painful, reevaluating his life and his priorities. Could anything be more risky for her than sharing in that?

Nuts. That's all. She was nuts and crazy and should have her head examined. Because even knowing all that, she'd lain in bed late into the night, wondering what it would be like to kiss him. To have his amazing hands touch her body. To make love to him.

She got into the shower, determined to do two things today: keep her distance from Guy and call her best friend, Allie, and ask for help.

CHAPTER NINE

"I CAN'T BE SURE, Dr. Browne, but this guy Stan sounds like someone I've run into before."

Rachel leaned forward in her chair, her gaze moving to the small notebook that was Heather's diary. She'd arrived at work early and read the whole thing, then she'd called Lieutenant Montgomery.

His Mississippi accent reminded her of a favorite professor she'd had in school, and she took to his easy manner immediately. When she'd mentioned Guy's name, he'd been very solicitous, and once she'd explained the circumstances surrounding Heather's death, he was downright kind.

She opened the notebook to the first page, where Guy had put the paper she'd found in Heather's coat pocket. "I have a phone number, although I have no idea if it's connected to Stan. It could be completely irrelevant. Guy called it a number of times, but there's no machine, and no answer."

"We'll check it out," the lieutenant said after she read him the number.

"It also occurred to us that Stan might have done this before. Getting girls pregnant and strung out, then disappearing. If that were the case, is there somewhere in the area these girls would go?"

She heard a slight tapping coming from the other end of the line. "I can think of a few places offhand. Let me call you back when I have more. Would that be all right?"

"Absolutely." She gave him all three of her numbers—home, cell and hospital.

"I'll call soon, Doctor."

"Call me Rachel, please. And thank you, Lieutenant."

"It's Richie, ma'am. Just plain old Richie. Now, you tell that bastard Giroux to take care of himself. We'll get to the bottom of this."

"Thank you." She hung up, but kept her hand on the phone. Before she could talk herself out of it, she'd dialed Allie's cell.

"'Lo."

"Allie?"

"Oh my God. It's the long-lost Rachel Browne. I thought you'd run away with the circus, girl. Where the hell have you been?"

Rachel leaned back, comforted at once by Allie's voice. "Working. And besides, it hasn't been that long."

"Two months? That's too long. What's up?"

"First, tell me how you are."

"I'm harried, but fine. Gerald is going crazy with the opening of the new gallery, and therefore, he has to drive me crazy."

"It'll be another smash, just like Longbow. The man has the best art connections in San Francisco—what can go wrong?"

"According to my darling hubby, everything."

"I know you'll soothe him through it all with your usual aplomb."

Allie chuckled. "Okay, now I know something's going on if you're buttering me up like this."

"I've got a situation."

"One that involves you getting laid a great deal, I hope?"

"No, not yet. I mean, no. Not getting laid. Not at all."

"Bummer."

"Allie…"

"Sorry. Continue."

"The situation does involve a man. Actually, a doctor."

"Okay, thanks for the distinction. That helps."

"He's my boss."

"Uh, let me fetch my coffee. This is getting better by the second."

Rachel waited until she heard Allie's "Okay, go."

"It's a long story."

"Lucky me, I've got a half hour until I have to meet a whole gang of attorneys who want to shut down a school for deaf kids. Nice, huh? But we can talk about that another time. Speak."

"His name is Guy Giroux, and he's the chief of the E.R. And he's had a bad personal loss. His stepdaughter died." Rachel laid out the facts, trying not to leave out anything pertinent. When she'd finished, there was a long pause.

"Uh, Rachel? That's all very interesting, but what's the problem?"

"The problem is, I like him."

"Ah."

"I can't like him. You know that. He's—"

"He's chipping away at those brick walls of yours, isn't he?"

Rachel sighed. "Yeah."

"And this is bad because…?"

"Allie, don't be obtuse."

"Right. *Feelings.* The forbidden zone."

"I didn't have to call you, you know."

"Okay, okay. I'll back off, but not totally. I've never really bought into your whole defense-mechanism theory, Rachel, and that's something *you* know. If you didn't want to hear my take, you wouldn't have called me."

Rachel winced. She'd known before she dialed the first number how this conversation was going to go, at least on some level. "What I need is a little help here. I don't think I'm going to be turning into someone else in the near future, so keep that in mind, okay?"

"You're helping him find this Stan person, right?"

"Yep."

"So use that. Take baby steps. When you talk to him, let the conversation happen. Feel what you feel. You don't have to act on anything, just be aware of it. When you're alone again, take those feelings out and look at them. See what seems right, what scares you. And then try to imagine what would happen if you took a *tiny* step out of your comfort zone."

Rachel brought her pencil up and stuck it between her teeth. "What kind of tiny step?"

"Well, what if you asked him to talk about this at your place? Over coffee."

"Oh, no. That'll be way over the line. He's my—"

"Boss, I know. But you had dinner at his house last night. That ship has sailed, my dear."

"Sailed. He has a boat, you know."

"Really?"

"Yeah. Loves it."

"Cool."

"Beside the point. I don't feel comfortable inviting him over."

"Okay, but you can still talk over coffee. And before you start giving him the lowdown—I mean, first thing— ask him how he's feeling."

Rachel bit the pencil.

"Don't freak on me, Rachel," Allie warned, as if she could see her friend. "All you have to do is listen to him. And respond with what your heart tells you."

"I can't get involved with him."

"I understand. But do it anyway. Hey, listen. What's going on with you next weekend?"

"Work."

"Can you spare a few hours for a long, no-holds-barred talk with your best buddy?"

"That would be great. I'll make sure I'm home and not on call."

"Cool. I'll buzz you later in the week when I know more about my schedule. Okay?"

"Great."

"And, honey?"

"What?"

"You're already involved with him. It's just a matter of degrees. So lighten up. This could be a good thing. With a capital *G*."

"More likely a nightmare with a capital *N*."

"Only if you want it that way. I've got to go. Remember, feelings are not the enemy. Bye."

Rachel put the phone in the cradle, thinking about what Allie had said. She'd told Rachel to listen to what was going on inside her, what made her afraid.

But Rachel already knew what made her afraid. On the other hand, maybe she should just shut up and do what she was told. Allie was one of the happiest people she knew. She was also damn good at her job, and she didn't live her life as if she'd break if something went wrong. So what the hell. Rachel would give it a try.

Right now, though, she had patients to tend to.

"TWO STAB WOUNDS to the left flank. First one is L2, 4 centimeters off the midline. Second one is L5, in the midscapular line."

Guy finished putting on his gloves as Brad Winslow, a fourth-year resident, gave him the vitals. He walked up to the patient, a young man, mid-twenties, pale and unconscious.

"Did it hit the spinal cord?" Theresa Finell, one of the best E.R. nurses asked, walking over to the patient. They were in trauma three, and since the only other patient in the hospital was a five-year-old who needed a couple of stitches, Guy had all the support he needed.

Winslow shook his head. "Depends on the angle."

Theresa took her place next to Guy. "BP's 70 over 50, pulse is 120."

"Squeeze in two liters and prepare for a subclavian," Guy said as he examined the man's chest. "What's his name?"

"John Gilliam. Stabbed in a bar fight."

Guy frowned. "Way to spend your afternoons, John."

"Good breath sounds bilaterally," Theresa said.

Guy went through the drill. "Ten liters by mask. Send a trauma panel, type and cross for 4 and get X ray in here for chest. And a one-shot IVP."

He moved down the table and flipped the white sheet from Gilliam's feet. "Toes are down going, so no spinal injury. Hang the next two units on the infuser."

For the next ten minutes, Guy barely looked up. The young man was in serious trouble. He needed surgery and he needed it now. "Book an O.R. Get ready to send him up. Where's the Foley?"

Theresa darted out of the room, and Guy tried not to be impatient.

"The one here got ripped, Doctor," Winslow said. "Theresa's getting a replacement. And pressure's up to 100 systolic."

"Give him a gram of cotetan."

The patient stirred, his eyes fluttering open.

Guy leaned over him. "John? Can you hear me? You're in a hospital. You've been stabbed, but we're taking care of you."

The boy looked at him with wild eyes. "My back."

"Hang in there. You're going up to surgery now."

Theresa ran in with a new Foley catheter and did a remarkably good job of getting it set up. But John didn't seem impressed; he was too busy moaning in pain.

"Dr. Giroux?"

He looked at Theresa.

She held up the Foley bag, and he saw it was filling with blood.

"Let's go. Make sure the O.R. is ready, Brad. Now."

Guy unlatched the gurney and pushed it out of the trauma room, heading toward the elevator.

He couldn't stop when he saw Rachel standing by the nurses' station. He'd have to catch up with her later.

RACHEL FINISHED writing her report on her last patient at seven-fifteen. She was tired and achy and she still hadn't heard from Lieutenant Montgomery. If she'd had her druthers, she would have gone straight home, crawled into a hot bubble bath and shut the world away.

But she still had to talk to Guy. The thought alone made her tense. Not just tense, truth be told. There was an element of excitement hidden in her jitters. Whether that was because she was going to try the Allie approach to listening, or because she just wanted to see him, she wasn't sure. Either way, thinking about it ratcheted up her stress level.

She headed toward his office, taking her day's reports with her. When she got to the reception area, Connie was on the phone. She held out a hand to stop Rachel, then pointed to a dish of butter cookies on the edge of her desk. Rachel couldn't resist. Connie was the best cook she knew. Well, except for Guy.

Rachel wondered how many women at the hospital knew about his culinary skills. She felt quite sure it was one of the many weapons in his arsenal. His looks, his charm, his profession, his boat. Good Lord, no woman stood a chance against him. And yet in the last few days he'd seemed more concerned with past failures than new conquests.

She'd read that people who had faced death head-on sometimes made amazing transformations. Although no one in her own experience had ever gone through anything so dramatic, death seemed to be a major trigger, as was a religious experience. She'd also heard that love could do it, but Rachel didn't believe that one.

Changing old habits was hard—one of the biggest challenges humans faced. Rachel doubted Guy was going to change permanently as a result of Heather's death. Given the life he had—success on every level, the career of his dreams—why would he?

For that matter, why should she?

She sat down in the soft visitor's chair and continued to nibble on her cookie. What Allie had asked her to do was change one of her own habits. To consciously let down the barriers and open herself up to Guy.

Sounded great on paper, but the barriers were there for a reason. She should know. She'd been in therapy, she'd examined her life, she'd faced the ugly truth. Her faults where cataloged and typed, cross-referenced and filed. Bottom line, they served her purposes, and she'd found no reason to rock the boat.

She realized the downside. People found her distant at times. She'd never win any popularity contests, and she'd felt the lack in her romantic life, but there were trade-offs in every endeavor. It was only lately that she'd started to wonder if this particular trade-off was worth it.

"Thanks for waiting," Connie said, hanging up the

phone. "He's on the line with the lab in San Francisco. As soon as he's off, you can go on in."

"These cookies are fantastic," Rachel said.

"Have another. You could use some meat on those bones."

"If I was around your cooking, I'd be big as a horse."

"No, you wouldn't, you'd be just as disciplined as you are about every other thing in your life. As for him—" she looked at Guy's closed door "—I hope you can take his mind off his troubles. I've never seen him so torn apart."

"I'll do what I can, Connie. But I'm not sure I'm the best person to help."

Connie studied Rachel with her dark, expressive gaze. "You can be. You just need to loosen up a little bit. Show that big heart of yours."

Rachel felt a twinge deep inside. Big heart? Where would Connie come up with that? When was the last time Rachel had done something that would be considered heartfelt?

She wasn't cold, but she wasn't like some of the other doctors here, who were so compassionate she'd worried they were crossing the line. Only, who was to say where that line should be drawn?

"Ah, he's off the phone," Connie told her. "You go on in. And take those cookies with you. I wish it was something healthier, but it's all I've got. I don't think he's eaten a bite all day."

"Thanks, Connie," Rachel said, taking the plate with her. She knocked on the door, but didn't wait for a reply before she entered the inner office.

"Hey," Guy said, smiling up at her from his desk.

"Hey, yourself." She put the cookies down. "Connie informs me you haven't eaten. She also says you should have something better than cookies."

He looked at the treats warily. "I'll get a bite at the cafeteria. Later."

She sat down, remembering Allie's words. For once she would repress her natural instincts to hold back. "How are you doing?"

He sighed. "I heard from Walter. Heather's father."

"Oh?"

"Bastard can't make it here until next week. Says he's in the middle of a business deal. Wanted to know about the funeral."

"What did you tell him?"

"That I'm waiting for Tammy. It's her decision."

"Is that all?"

Leaning back in his chair, he stared up at the wall behind her. He looked tired, defeated. And so sad. "I gave him a few choice thoughts. Useless, of course."

"So forget about him. Tell me what's going on with Heath."

"He's stabilized. But it's not great. He's probably going to need an operation on his heart, but right now it's his kidney function that's paramount... You know the drill. I'm just grateful at this point that he's hanging on."

Rachel looked down at her hands, at the manicure she'd had yesterday. The blatant honesty coming from Guy made her think of five excuses to leave. She wasn't used to this casual frankness from him. It disarmed her and made her feel vulnerable. But she'd keep going, testing this new ground. She raised her gaze and took a deep breath. "It has to be very hard for you."

"It is. I never had a child of my own, but this…" He leaned forward, his eyes moist. "Nothing can happen to him, Rachel."

"He's getting the best care possible."

"I know. But I can't—" His voice broke.

She stood up, went to his side and crouched down next to him, touching his arm gently. "You can't be the one. I know. You're used to being the doctor. The one who pulls the rabbit out of the hat. The person who saves lives despite all the odds. The people looking after Heath are the very best in the field, Guy, and they're going to move heaven and earth to save him. All you can do now is love him."

Guy opened his mouth, but nothing came out. No words at all, and yet she understood his anguish, his frustration. Perhaps it was only something doctors could feel when all their education, all their training meant nothing.

But there was something more, something that made her pulse quicken in fear. The way he looked at her wasn't simply as a man in pain, but a man in need. A man who needed her. It was as if he was calling out to her, screaming to her to save him.

"Oh, God, Guy. I can't—"

He leaned toward her and put his hand on hers. "Rachel." His gaze raked her face, and the intensity of his expression took her breath. It was as if he could see inside her. Deep into her secrets.

And then he moved closer still, close enough that she felt his warm breath caress her cheek and she could see the flecks of gold in the depths of his eyes.

His lips touched hers, so gently, and she closed her eyes, trying not to bolt. She wanted to let herself feel— the texture of his lips, the tenderness, the way his hand squeezed hers so tightly. His need for her was in his touch, in his breath.

When he rose, he brought her up with him, his kiss deepening as his hand left hers and slipped to the back of her neck. He pulled her against him, and she was swamped by the physical sensations swirling inside her.

Her hands moved up his back, and for this moment, she was with him, trying to give him comfort. She'd never wanted to be so much to one person. Healing this way was completely foreign to her.

"Oh, that's just great."

Rachel jumped back at the intrusive voice, her face burning and every part of her shutting down. She didn't recognize the woman standing just inside Guy's office.

Guy sighed. "Tammy."

"You can't even wait till she's buried?" His ex-wife walked inside, her fury making her seem much taller than her diminutive frame.

Blond, beautiful, dressed in tight black leather pants and a red, low-cut sweater, she looked like the perfect trophy wife. Her makeup was flawless and not a hair was out of place, but her anger was palpable as her gaze moved from Guy to Rachel and back. "You have to do your whore right here, in your office? In the same hospital where that little baby lies dying?"

CHAPTER TEN

"YOU LOOK GREAT, Tammy," Guy said. "I hate that you had to come home to this."

Tammy seemed taken aback at Guy's calm. "This isn't my home."

Guy turned to Rachel, and with a sad smile said, "Would you excuse us, please?"

"Of course." She walked around his desk. When she stood next to Tammy, she paused. "I'm so sorry for your loss."

Tammy grunted, looking away from Rachel as quickly as possible. Taking the cue, Rachel left, alarmed that the door was open and the crude remarks would have been heard by Connie.

Rachel didn't even glance at Guy's secretary as she hurried out of the reception area. It wasn't embarrassment at Tammy's outburst that mortified her, but her own culpability.

She'd kissed Guy Giroux.

Allie would have been thrilled, no doubt, but Rachel was anything but. She'd kissed Guy, in his office. Kissed him and felt...

Felt too much.

She hurried to her office and got her purse and coat, then left the hospital as quickly as she could. Once in her car, she burned rubber heading out of the parking lot, determined to escape, but the lingering effects of what she'd done grew stronger the closer she got to home.

There was compassion and then there was stupidity, and she'd leaped over the boundary with both feet. Yes, the man needed a friend, but *kissing?*

Even when she pulled into her garage and the door closed behind her, she didn't move, just sat with both hands on the wheel, staring at the speedometer.

She'd been knocked off balance, and she wasn't sure how to regain her footing. This was someone else's life, not her own. Connie had been right. Rachel was disciplined, especially when it came to work. She simply didn't do foolish things, and there was no doubt in her mind that kissing Guy was foolish in the extreme.

The real kicker was that she'd liked it. What a stupid word that was: *like.* It didn't come close to the feelings that had hit her the moment his lips touched hers.

Closing her eyes, she struggled to find the words to quantify the experience. But instead of an easy explanation, the quiver in her stomach came back, the tingles where he'd brushed the back of her neck, the breathlessness that had made her dizzy. It all came back, leaving her adrift, afloat on an unfamiliar sea.

This was ridiculous. She got out of the car, slamming the door shut. She wasn't a virgin. She'd been with men, had sex. Not often, and not in a long time, but she was hardly chaste and pure. The kiss was nothing, one tiny step above a peck on the cheek.

Once inside the house, she turned on the light in the kitchen. Everything was tidy, no dishes on the counter, the bouquet of roses still fresh in the crystal vase on the dining room table. The room was exactly how she'd left it this morning, yet somehow it now seemed sterile, cold.

That was also ridiculous.

She hung her coat up in the hall closet, then headed to her bedroom. Once there, she unpinned her hair and let it fall down her back. Then she went to the bathroom and prepared a bubble bath, using her favorite freesia oil. Next came music, and she chose Debussy, turning up the volume before she took off her clothes.

Naked, she lit the candles, all six of them, put her towels within reaching distance, and climbed into the almost too warm water.

It took her a minute to get settled, to adjust the bath pillow behind her head and stir the oils and the bubbles to perfection.

Then she turned off the tap, lay back, closed her eyes and listened to *Clair de Lune,* letting the exquisite music take her away. Away from her thoughts, away from the confusion of Guy Giroux.

But not for long. Not nearly long enough. She couldn't block him out, nor could she erase the imprint of his kiss.

She was adrift, all right, and she had no idea how to get back to shore.

TAMMY SAT with her coffee, both of them still steaming. She looked good, better than she had the last time

Guy had seen her. France agreed with her, or perhaps now she was finally free to be the woman she'd always wanted to be. An artist, she had actually completed and sold several works.

Guy was curious about it. He'd never been able to picture that. Her art had seemed an affectation when they were together, something she dreamed about but never actualized. Leaving him, it appeared, had been the key. He felt odd, sitting across from her now. It was as if he were looking at a stranger instead of a woman who had once shared his life.

He had never shared her life, though. Except for Heather. But that wasn't the truth, either, was it? He had kept Heather, like Tammy, on the periphery. There hadn't been room in his world for them.

"She never said a word to me," Tammy told him, apparently still wrapped in the guilt of her neglect. "She told me she was with Walter. That she was having a good time. Going to movies, hanging out with her friends."

"Did she ever mention names? Who those friends might be?"

Tammy shook her head. Her hair, blonder now than when he'd been with her, shimmered on her shoulders. It was a good look for her, softening her cheekbones and sharp jaw. Her makeup was more subdued, too. "Just friends," she said. "Just stuff. The last couple of years she'd gotten vague, distant. I thought it was a phase. She was a teenager, for God's sake. This was supposed to be her year of fun before college. We talked about that." Tammy blinked tears from her eyes. "She wanted to go to UCLA. Her SATs were really good. She'd been accepted."

"I didn't know that."

"Of course not." She put her cup on his desk and crossed her legs. "When was the last time you talked to her?"

"Too long ago," he said. He wasn't going to excuse himself. Not to Tammy and not to himself. "I didn't think enough about her."

"No, you didn't. She loved you."

"I know."

"Do you? Did you know she used to ask me about you every time we talked? She told me one of the things she wanted to do while she was with Walter was to come stay with you for a while."

"No. I had no idea. She never called."

"Well, no, she wouldn't. She was too busy getting pregnant." Tammy lost the battle with her tears. She reached into her purse and brought out a crumpled tissue. "God, who was he? What did he do to her?"

"I'm doing my best to find out. I've made some calls."

"To whom?"

"I don't know if you remember him, but I used to sail with a policeman from the LAPD. Richie Montgomery."

She shook her head. "I hated all those stupid sailing parties."

She hadn't, in fact. Not always. In the beginning, when they'd lived in L.A., Tammy had loved the parties, the regattas, the Sundays at the marina. She'd entertained like a true hostess. The champagne had been too expensive, the caviar imported, the caterers in their bright white jackets. She'd eaten it up. It was only when she had to live here, in the quiet of Courage Bay, that she'd learned to hate everything about him, including his boat.

"Richie will do what he can to help," Guy said. "He's a good man."

"His name was Stan?"

Guy nodded.

"And he got her on drugs?"

He nodded again.

"Is that why…?"

"No, at least not for the most part. Heath has a genetic illness, as far as we can tell."

"What the hell does that mean?"

"It means that we're still doing tests. These things aren't simple. There are so many conditions. If it is what we think, then it's serious but not fatal."

"Don't give me that doctorspeak, Guy. Tell me what you know."

"We think Heath might have Noonan's syndrome. But we have to wait to find out for sure."

"And if he does?"

"Then he'll need a special kind of care for the rest of his life. He may not develop normally. He might exhibit traits similar to Down's syndrome, and his physical condition will be…difficult."

Tammy's eyes closed, and he noticed her hands were trembling in her lap. It must seem so unfair to her to have this happen to her ordered life. Now that she'd finally found herself, she was going to have to give it all up to care for Heath. *If* she decided to take him. She could also give him up for adoption.

The thought chilled Guy to the bone. Finding someone to care for Heath would be a challenge. He knew
there were people who took special-needs children into
their lives, but there were so many children out there.

The bottom line was that Tammy was the child's
closest relative. Tammy and Walter. But there wasn't a
chance in hell that Walter was going to lift a finger to
help the boy. He'd barely acknowledged his own daughter, let alone a bastard grandson.

Guy just hoped Tammy would take some time, consider all the options. He prayed that Heath would live
long enough for her to fall in love with him.

Tammy's head came up, her eyes dry now and fired
up with anger. "So who was she?"

"Pardon?"

"Don't even start."

"She's a friend, Tammy. A co-worker."

"She's a nurse?"

"A doctor. A fine one. She's an attending physician
in the E.R."

"Isn't that a little too close, even for you?"

"It's not like that."

"Oh? From where I stood, it was very much like that.
Or do you make out with all your attendings?"

He smiled, working at keeping a lid on his temper.
She wasn't making it easy. "Knock it off, Tammy. We
aren't married anymore. We haven't been for years.
What I do is my business."

She looked at him with such palpable disdain he felt
dirty. "You haven't changed a bit. Not one bit. Still the
most selfish bastard I've ever met."

"Yep, that's me." He stood up and pushed his chair into the desk. "Do you want to see your grandchild, or would you prefer to keep harping at me?"

Tammy winced, and he tried to care. "Yes, I want to see him."

He headed to the door, not even looking back to see if she was behind him. Connie had gone home a while ago. As he led Tammy to the elevator, he glanced at the E.R. He knew Rachel had also gone home, and he wondered if she was as nonplussed by what had happened as he was. Not Tammy's unfortunate timing, but before that.

When he'd kissed her... God, he hadn't expected anything like that. She hadn't been just another woman in his arms, another conquest. He'd felt—

"Are you coming?"

He realized he was standing outside the elevator, and that Tammy was holding the door. He walked inside, unwilling to think about Rachel or that kiss while he was with Tammy. Especially now. Despite her vindictiveness, he had to remember what a difficult time she was having. Seeing Heath wasn't going to be any kind of a comfort, and accepting that Heather would never know her son would be a special form of hell.

On the fourth floor, Tammy slowed her pace. She still twisted the tissue in her right hand, while her left clutched her purse like a lifeline.

"We need to scrub up, put on a mask before we can see him."

"Is he contagious?"

"No, but we are. The children in here are highly susceptible to any airborne illness. Every precaution is taken not to introduce foreign bacteria."

She watched him wash and followed suit, and then he put the mask over her mouth and nose. He took her to Heath's incubator, although she stopped a few feet away.

He understood. It wasn't easy to see such a tiny creature in so much distress. Even though every piece of equipment was scaled down to preemie size, the effect was still overwhelming.

Heath's jaundice had diminished, but his weight hadn't improved. He looked impossibly small, and the tiny wool cap on his head almost covered his eyes.

What worried Guy the most was the infant's lack of mobility. Heath was so still that if Guy hadn't been looking at the monitors, if he hadn't been able to read the heart rhythm, he would have thought Heath was a terrible doll, not a living child.

From behind him, he heard Tammy's gasp, and a moan that came from the deepest part of her heart. He turned and pulled her into his arms and just held her for a long, long time, while she wept for all that was lost, all that would never be.

RACHEL HUNG UP, but kept her hand on the phone. She looked at the clock by her bed. Almost eleven-thirty. Guy was probably asleep. At least he should be. But the information Lieutenant Montgomery had given her was the first hopeful thing that had happened since Heather's death.

She lifted the phone and dialed his home number. At the third ring, she went to hang up, but his voice stopped her. "Did I wake you?" she asked.

"Rachel." The way he said her name made her bring her legs up to her chest and hug them tight. "No, you didn't wake me. I just got home."

"Oh."

"I'm sorry about that introduction this afternoon. Tammy isn't so bad. It's just a rough time for her."

"Yeah, I imagine it is. How about you?"

He laughed, although there was no humor in it. "Today wasn't pretty. But Tammy's safe in her hotel room. She's said all the things she wanted to say, and I think tomorrow might be a little easier on both of us."

"And Heath?"

"He's the same. She wasn't prepared, of course. How could she be."

"It's going to be tough."

"I think we're all going to be taking this one step at a time."

"Sure."

"Are you all right?"

"Me? Oh, yeah." She shifted her position and slid under the covers, bringing them high up on her chest. "I got a call from your friend."

"Richie?"

"Yes. He knows who Stan is."

She heard his sharp intake of breath, then nothing for several heartbeats. "Who is he?"

"His name is Stan DiGrasso, and he's wanted for possession and distribution of drugs. He's been in trouble for years, and he's brought a lot of people down with him."

"Mostly, I'm guessing, young girls."

"That's not official, but yes. Montgomery believes he can connect DiGrasso to three other young women. But he can't find any of them. They all just vanished. Their parents have no idea what happened to them. It's not good."

"Does he know where DiGrasso is?"

"No, although he does believe he's still in Los Angeles. They're going after one of his sources. The drugs are the only way they know how to track him down."

Again, there was silence, and Rachel pictured Guy standing in his beautiful kitchen. She knew he had to be exhausted beyond belief, and the kindest thing she could do would be hang up and talk to him tomorrow. But she'd already made the mistake of calling, so she'd wait until he said goodbye.

"There might be another way," Guy said.

"What do you mean?"

"If he's fathered other children with these women, then there must be hospital records. If even one of those kids inherited the disorder, he or she would need a tremendous amount of care."

"Of course. Hospital records of anyone born in the last five years with Noonan's."

"We can get that here, then when I'm in L.A...."

"You can try and track him from the records."

"Yeah, right. Listen. Tammy made her decision about Heather."

"I'm sorry, what?"

"I know I'm switching gears here, but bear with me, okay?"

"Sure."

"Heather's going to be buried in Los Angeles."

"Oh, my. Why?"

"Tammy has friends there. Walter's there."

"When?"

"The day after tomorrow."

"That's good. You can investigate while you're there."

"That's exactly what I was thinking. If we can do the traces tomorrow, there's a chance I can track him down."

She smiled. Guy needed something to do, something positive that would make him feel as if he was making a difference. Getting that bastard would fit the bill nicely. It would be the only good thing about his trip. Burying his stepdaughter would be harder than anything she could imagine.

"Rachel?"

"Yeah?"

"Come with me."

She laughed. "Guy, come on. Don't be silly. I have to work, you know that."

"I can get someone to cover for you."

"You'll already be gone. Won't that leave us in the lurch?"

"I'm serious, I can make sure we're covered. That's not an issue."

"But if I go with you, who's going to watch Heath?"

He didn't say anything for a while, and she figured he must have realized how absurd it was to even think she could go with him to Los Angeles.

"You were right—what you said this afternoon. He's in the best possible hands. And as I found out tonight, I'm actually not helping matters."

"What do you mean?"

"Now that Tim Burns is back, he told me the best thing I can do for Heath right now is to let him do his job. My second-guessing every procedure is making everyone on the team nervous."

"*I'm* not making them crazy."

"But you're making me uncrazy."

She had no idea how to respond to that. She tried to say something, but gave up.

"Today, when you were…there," Guy began, "I felt, I don't know, at peace…for the first time since this all began. In fact, it's not just today. I can't explain it. I just know it's true. I need you to come with me, Rachel. I'll get us separate rooms. This isn't about what Tammy said. I'm not going to seduce you. It's about… I need a friend. And I'd be more grateful than you can ever know if you'd consider coming with me."

Rachel pulled the phone away and stared at it, as if it had sprouted wings. She knew Guy meant what he was saying, but she didn't believe she could be whatever it was he wanted her to be.

To leave work was out of the question. She hadn't missed a day in over a year.

To leave work to go to L.A. with Guy was… Well, it just couldn't happen.

Okay, she felt something for him, but come on. This was nuts. He was in pain, that's all. Confused. It was a devastating time for him, and his thinking was all over the map.

"Rachel?"

She brought the phone back to her ear as she shook her head. "I'm sorry, Guy. It's just not a good idea."

"I know. But I'm asking you to do it anyway."

Rachel closed her eyes and sighed. Then she heard Allie's voice in the back of her mind telling her she was a chicken. A wimp. A coward. Allie would have pooh-poohed all the completely legitimate reasons for saying no, and she would have said it was good for Rachel to risk this. Allie would never let her live it down if she said no.

Rachel opened her eyes again. "All right, I'll go," she said. "But only if I'm absolutely certain the E.R. is covered."

It was crazy, but she could have sworn she heard him smile.

CHAPTER ELEVEN

THE AUTOPSY SUITE at Courage Bay Hospital was a meticulous white, and Callie Baker noted with approval that the morgue technician and the pathologist were well into Bruce Nepom's autopsy when she arrived. She'd asked to be present for the examination of the skull and brain, and from the looks of things, it would be another twenty or thirty minutes before that procedure would begin.

Just as she was about to go outside and call Chief Zirinsky, the door behind her opened. Max had a white gown on over his uniform. He looked strikingly handsome, especially when he smiled at her.

"I knew I shouldn't have had breakfast before I came here," he said.

"After all these years, you're not used to autopsies?"

He shook his head. "It's a miracle I don't embarrass myself."

"I remember a few when you looked pretty green."

He shook his head, but took the jab with good humor. "So what are you thinking on this, Callie?"

"I'm anxious to see the back of his skull and the damage done to the posterior of the brain."

"You'll be able to tell if the injury was caused by something other than a falling roof?"

"I should, yes." She walked closer to the autopsy table. Nepom's body had already been cleared of internal organs, and the body block had been removed from underneath his back. The pathologist, Ralph Kushner, who'd been with Courage Bay Hospital for almost ten years, nodded her way.

"We're doing the brain now, Doctor," he said.

Nepom's head was elevated and Kushner used his scalpel to reveal the skull. Typically, he would cut the skull now to reveal the brain, but instead, he exposed the back area so that he and Callie could look at the damage.

As she suspected, there was a deep concussion just above the brain stem, with a large portion of the skull shattered. "There," she said to Max. "That was the result of a heavy blow by a blunt instrument. A hammer or a pipe. But my money's on a hammer."

Max cursed softly, taking out a notebook that he had in his breast pocket. "You'll get me the report ASAP?"

"Of course."

The pathologist went on to remove the brain, and it amazed Callie that Nepom had lived as long as he had. "You know anything about him?" she asked Max.

"Not much, but I have a feeling I'm going to get to know Mr. Nepom real well."

"There's one other thing I wanted to show you," she said, moving down to Nepom's arm. She held it up, her white gloves so clean-looking next to the man's weathered skin. "This tattoo."

Max looked at it carefully and made another notation in his book. "Can you get a picture of that for me?"

Callie glanced at the morgue technician. "Will you take care of that, Dell? Send me the pictures along with the report."

"Sure thing, Dr. Baker," he said, heading to the side cupboards where they kept the camera equipment.

"Is there anything else?" She put Nepom's arm down carefully before turning to Max.

"No, I think that pretty much says it all. Do you have any idea about directionality of the blow?"

"It looked to me as if it came down from the left."

"Great. Listen, I have to get to a meeting. But I appreciate you calling me in on this."

"Let me know if there's anything else I can do."

He nodded. "Thank you, gentlemen," he said, although he didn't wait for a response. Callie couldn't blame him for leaving as quickly as he could. Autopsies were tough for anyone. She watched him walk out of the room, but just before the door closed behind him, he turned to her, as if he was going to say something else, then simply smiled and left.

Callie turned back to the body, watching as the pathologist went inch by inch over the brain, the skull and the blunt-force trauma that had killed Bruce Nepom.

GUY WAITED until Connie had finished writing before he put down his coffee. "Have I forgotten anything?"

"Don't think so," she said, reviewing her notes. "We've got everything covered here, even if you're gone a week."

"I won't be. Three days, at the most. Probably two. The funeral is tomorrow, and we should be able to find out what we can about Stan the following day."

"I'm just saying you don't need to worry. The E.R. is looked after, and Dr. Burns is going to be with Heath. I'll check on the baby regularly, so all you have to do is call me for an update."

Guy stood up, feeling guilty about leaving the boy. "You're sure?"

"Doctor, everyone on staff has a particular fondness for that little guy. We'll watch him as if he were our own."

"I know that, Connie, and I appreciate it more than I can say. I wouldn't be leaving if I didn't believe it."

"You have important things to do. And what else is there but to do them?"

Guy smiled, appreciating Connie more than ever. "I know it's probably hopeless, but maybe you can stem the rumor tide about Rachel. She's being a real friend here, and she doesn't need to go through the gossip mill."

Connie folded her steno book, then stood. "It's too late. But I'll do my best to feed the truth in there somehow."

The phone rang, and Connie answered. She frowned, then handed it to Guy. "I'll get to work on these schedules," she said, heading for the door.

"Hello?"

"I've talked to Walter," Tammy said, eschewing any pleasantries. "The service is at eleven at Forest Lawn."

"I'll be there," he said.

"I don't see any reason for me to stay, so I'll be catching a plane tonight. Walter will get me from the airport."

Guy's gut tightened with anger, but he held back, not

wanting to start anything now. No reason to stay? What about her grandson? Screw it, he thought. "Are you coming to see Heath before you leave?"

She hesitated long enough for him to know she hadn't considered Heath in her plans. "Of course."

"Have you given any thought to what you're going to do after the funeral?"

"No. I haven't. But you'll be the first to know when I do."

His hand gripped the phone so tightly he felt as if it would crumble to dust. "Fine. I'll see you later."

She didn't even say goodbye, which was just as well, because he'd run flat out of civility. God, that woman made him insane.

It was time to do rounds. The E.R. was pretty quiet, but there were still patients to be seen. And Rachel.

He still couldn't quite believe he'd asked her to go to Los Angeles and that she'd said yes. He hoped she hadn't changed her mind.

The only problem was his promise to her. It had plagued him all last night. He'd told her he wanted her there as a friend, and God knows that was true. But as for the part about not seducing her? That might prove to be a challenge.

He got his stethoscope from behind his door and wrapped it around his neck. Connie was on the phone and didn't even look up at him as he headed toward the E.R. The sound of an ambulance coming into the bay set his adrenaline pumping. He'd never really thought about it, but he was so conditioned to the sounds of the hospital. A code, a siren, the beep of a monitor—his response was Pavlovian, and it happened outside the hospital, as well. His body was trained to respond, and even now, though he didn't have a clue what to expect, the initial treatment procedures were running through his head.

The truth was, medicine was in his blood. He'd been at it for over twenty years. Days, nights, weeks, months and years, seeing every form of trauma that could befall a human, and yet there were still surprises, still challenges every day. Or there would be, if he hadn't been so bogged down with administrative duties.

He loved so much about the work. It defined him. When he'd become chief of the E.R., he'd had everything he ever wanted.

So why the questions? Why had Heather's death and Heath's birth spun him into such turmoil?

By the time he got to the ambulance entrance, Rachel was already there, listening to the EMT as he rattled off the patient's condition. A car accident, a bad one.

"He's pink, warm, slightly diaphoretic," the paramedic said, carrying a bag of saline as they wheeled the patient to trauma one. "Heart rate tachy at 110. Respirations also tachy at 27. Temp normal at 97.9."

As soon as they were in the room, on the count of three, the patient was transferred to the bed.

"I need two large-bore IVs," Rachel said, her voice steady and calm. "Call X ray, we need STAT c-spine clearance in order to take the patient off the board. Katya, get the Foley. Solumedrol 2 grams IV bolus."

Guy didn't interfere, although he paid close attention

to Rachel as she continued to guide her team, covering all the bases.

His focus shifted from the patient to Rachel herself. It was like watching an athlete in her prime, or an artist. Every move had meaning, and there was no waste, no hesitation.

The supporting players followed her commands with complete confidence, and the process went smoothly. The woman was born to do this. Like Guy, Rachel's work defined her. He understood that part of her in a way that only another E.R. doctor could. But there was more to her than her trauma skills. And that part remained a mystery, one worth investigating.

The question was, would Rachel let him close enough to do that? She was the most private person he'd ever known. It wasn't just him, either. No one at the hospital knew much about her, although Connie had some interesting insights.

Mostly, Connie believed Rachel was one of the good guys. And for Connie, that was saying a lot. Her instincts about people were startlingly accurate. When Connie didn't trust someone, Guy kept his ears sharp and his back protected, and ten times out of ten, she'd been right on the money.

His own instincts had led him to hire Rachel, and he'd never been sorry. But he'd also respected her privacy and never, until these last few days, considered pursuing anything more than a professional relationship.

Now all he wanted was for Rachel to open up. To tell him everything about herself. And he wanted to make love to her.

He stepped back, shocked at the power of his desire. Knowing Rachel had the situation well in hand, he continued rounds, needing some distance.

What had triggered this reaction to a woman he'd known for so long? The turnaround was unprecedented, unlike anything he'd ever experienced.

His reaction to women had always been immediate and primitive. It wasn't one thing that drew him, but a combination. Of course, looks counted in a woman, although his tastes were varied. More critical was that she was bright, inquisitive, adventurous.

He knew Rachel was smart as a whip, and that she approached the world as a student as well as a teacher. But she'd never given him any indication she'd been interested in him. Maybe that was it. He wanted what he couldn't have. Needed a challenge to take his mind off—

Shit. He really was a shallow bastard. In it for himself, and nothing else mattered. Tammy had him nailed. If he had any decency at all, he'd tell Rachel to forget it, that he could manage in L.A. by himself.

RACHEL STRIPPED OFF her bloody gloves and lab coat and dumped them into the biowaste unit at the edge of the trauma room. Her body ached in a too-familiar way after hours of concentrated focus. It seemed as if she'd used every muscle and absolutely all of her brain function. Coffee and a rest beckoned, but not yet. She still had to talk to the patient's wife.

She'd known after the first five minutes that the man would never walk again. His spinal cord had been so severely injured that he was lucky to have any feeling at all in his hands. Maybe after extensive therapy, he'd be able to hold a cup or brush his teeth.

His wife was in the waiting room. A pretty woman, so very young. And there was a child, too. A little girl who would grow up with her father in a wheelchair. They'd never play ball together or take a walk to the corner store.

The prospect of telling them what their future looked like chilled Rachel to the bone. She didn't want to witness the horror as Mrs. Wilson started to comprehend that nothing in her life would ever be the same. If she was lucky, the marriage would last and she would form a deeper relationship with her husband. But if she was like most women, the marriage would be over in about three years.

Rachel hoped she could help.

Just days ago, the concept of offering kindness wouldn't have crossed her mind. In fact, she'd have been appalled at involving her own feelings at all. Her job was to tell the truth, to give the family options, including who to go to for counseling. Certainly not her. She'd done her magic in trauma one. She'd saved the man's life. She'd done everything medically possible to make sure he'd get maximum use of his body. That was her gift, not compassion.

Steeling herself, she put on a clean lab coat and headed toward the waiting room.

Mrs. Wilson and her child, a little girl Rachel guessed to be around five, were alone. There was a blizzard of torn tissues scattered across the fake-leather seat, and several pieces on the floor. The little girl was wearing a pink jumper with tiny white tennis shoes and carried a doll with wild blond hair.

Mrs. Wilson looked at Rachel with such hope that her resolve wavered. Her chest constricted and hot tears burned her eyes.

Turning away, Rachel struggled to get herself under control. The last thing this woman needed was a weepy doctor. She needed strength for the long road ahead, and damn it, Rachel was going to give it to her.

After slipping off her stethoscope and putting it in her pocket, Rachel walked slowly into the room and mustered her most reassuring smile. She sat down, close enough to the woman that she would be able to speak softly. Far enough away that they wouldn't touch.

As Rachel began to explain what had happened, it was everything she could do to keep her voice steady, her eyes clear. The pain in her heart was like a scalpel, cutting past all the defenses she'd built year after year, tragedy after tragedy.

This was why she couldn't let go. Why she had to keep her distance. Because when the walls came down, all they revealed was her weakness. Her terribly human, achingly flawed weakness.

It didn't matter that through her tears, Mrs. Wilson thanked her. It didn't matter that she leaned across the distance and hugged Rachel tight. What mattered was that Rachel had, from the moment she walked in, stopped being a doctor and become an emotional woman. Who couldn't help anyone. No one at all.

"WHO IS THIS?"

Rachel sniffed, wiped her nose, then turned her head back to the phone. "It's me."

"Rachel?"

She nodded.

"Rachel, what happened? Speak, damn it. I can't hear you if you don't say anything."

"Allie, I made a big mistake."

"What? Did someone die?"

"No, it's nothing like that. No one died."

"Thank God. So what's this big mistake?"

Rachel started crying again, and she had to turn her chair in case someone walked into her office. She couldn't stand it if anyone from the hospital saw her this way.

"Honey? Rachel? Please, stop crying and just tell me what happened."

"Hold on." Rachel put the phone down and plucked two more tissues from the box. She blew her nose as hard as she could, then picked up the phone again. "I said yes."

"Uh, you said yes to who?"

"Whom."

"Great, let's call the grammar police. I'm sure they can help."

"Sorry."

"Okay. So you said yes to whom?"

"Guy."

"Rachel, stop crying. Take a deep breath. You can do it. I know you can."

Rachel obeyed, and in a minute, she was calmer, although no happier. "Okay."

"What did you say yes to?"

"He asked me to go with him to Los Angeles. To his stepdaughter's funeral. And to help find the guy that got her pregnant."

"Oh."

"What the hell does that mean?" Rachel asked, her eyes welling with tears once again. She plucked another tissue from the box.

"Well, give me a second," Allie said. "I'm trying to process here."

"You have one minute."

"Gee, thanks. At least tell me why you're crying."

"I just told you."

"Nope. Not buying that. Try again."

"Damn you."

"I love you, too. Now come on. Why?"

"Because this guy, he was hurt in a car accident."

"Bad?"

"He'll never walk again."

"Ouch."

"And when I went to talk to his wife and his little girl…" Her throat closed up.

"I'll wait," Allie said, her voice ten degrees calmer.

Finally, Rachel could speak again. "I was a wreck," she confessed. "I cried. I felt horrible for her. All I could see was that little girl trying to understand why her daddy couldn't pick her up. How they were going to have to change their house, and that nothing would ever be the same again. And how strong everyone was going to have to be, and that most marriages don't make it when something like this happens, and she was this really nice woman, and her little girl was named Alice."

Allie's breath came in a whoosh over the phone. "Oh, my."

"It was awful."

"Rachel?"

She sniffed. "What?"

"I need you to do something for me."

"What?"

"I need you to listen."

"I'm listening."

"No, you're not. You're dumping, which is fine, but now I need you to calm yourself down and listen to what I'm going to say."

Rachel wanted to argue, but she didn't. She just breathed as deeply as she could, letting out the air slowly. Allie had always been her rock, her safety net, and when it came to relationships, no one did it better. Allie would know what to do.

When Rachel was just shy of hyperventilating, she said, "Okay, I'm listening."

"Good. Because, sweetie, it wasn't awful. It was fantastic."

"Allie—"

"What did I say?"

Rachel closed her eyes and tried hard not to curse. "Fine. Go on."

"Okay. Here's the thing. You felt something today you haven't let yourself feel for a long time. And you got through it."

"But I cried!"

"So what? You got through it. You told the woman what she needed to hear. And I'd be willing to bet my entire year's salary that she was incredibly grateful that you cared, Rachel. That you could see and understand her pain."

"No. She needed a doctor, not a wuss."

"Who made the rule that a doctor can't be a wuss? It happens all the time. With the best of them, that is."

Rachel's hand froze halfway to her nose. "Are you saying I haven't been a good doctor?"

"You're the best technician I know. I'd rather have you operate on me than anyone else in the world."

"But?"

"I'd rather have the candy striper tell me the prognosis."

Rachel didn't answer. She couldn't. This was her best friend—her only real friend—telling her she was more of a machine than a person. A technician with no soul. "It hurt too much, Allie," she whispered.

"I know. And it always will. But please, Rachel, do yourself the biggest favor of your life. Go to Los Angeles with Guy. Please. If you've never trusted me before, trust me now. Go to L.A."

Rachel stared at the wall behind her desk as she hung the phone delicately on the cradle.

CHAPTER TWELVE

GUY RESTED AGAINST the back door of the elevator on the short ride from the fourth floor to the first. Alone at last, with Heath comfortably sleeping and Tammy on her way to the airport. He couldn't remember being more exhausted. There were only a few things he had to do before he could go home.

The elevator came to a gliding stop and he walked into the brightly lit hallway. Following the red line, he made his way back to the trauma rooms, but Rachel wasn't there. She wasn't in her office, either. He knew she hadn't gone home, so he got back on the elevator and went down to the basement. To the left was the morgue and the autopsy bay, to the right, around the corner, the cafeteria. He headed right.

Rachel was at a small table at the far end of the room, by herself, staring at her plate.

Along with the civilians, there were several nurses, one of the pharmacists and a couple of guys from maintenance occupying the pale blue plastic tables. The mural on the wall was a scene from Courage Bay's history. It showed the sailors being rescued from their ship by the local Indian tribe. In fact, one of the sailors depicted was his ancestor, Pierre Giroux. Guy didn't see any resemblance.

He started toward Rachel, but the grumbling in his stomach reminded him that he hadn't eaten in a hell of a long time, so he checked out the food line. Neither clam chowder nor vegetable beef soup appealed, and he didn't want a salad, either. Instead, he got some meat loaf, which was one of the best things on the menu, mashed potatoes and steamed broccoli. There was still some room on his tray, so he grabbed a piece of apple pie.

After paying, he headed straight toward Rachel's table. She jumped when he said, "Hello."

"May I?"

She pushed her tray to the side. "Sit."

He did, and another wave of exhaustion hit him, making the act of eating seem like a Herculean effort. "You haven't eaten much."

She looked at the barely touched lasagna and green salad on her plate. "I'm not very hungry."

He folded his napkin on his lap and studied her subdued expression. "What's wrong?"

"Nothing."

"Hmm."

She arched an eyebrow. "What's that supposed to mean?"

"Just that you don't look like nothing's wrong. I'm hoping you feel comfortable enough with me to let me know if I'm right."

When she didn't answer, he took a few bites of meat and potatoes. Finally, she sighed, poking her fork into her pasta. "Did you find out any information about hospitals?" she asked.

Guy nodded. "Three. One hospital had three babies with the same symptoms. All the births took place within the past five years. But I ended up with only one address on Stan DiGrasso, although they were going to keep digging."

"But that's a start, right?"

"Right."

She nibbled on a piece of lettuce.

"So okay," he said. "I won't press it. We can talk about Stan some more if you like."

The look Rachel gave him said she was on to his tactics and wasn't sure she wanted to play. But then she put the fork down and stared him straight in the eye. "I'm debating the wisdom of joining you in Los Angeles."

He swallowed, then cleared his throat. He wasn't surprised, just disappointed. Yeah, he'd initially talked himself out of inviting her, but damn it, now that she was saying no, he realized how much he was counting on her being with him. "Any particular reason?"

"Lots. Starting with my number-one rule."

"Which is?"

"Not dating anyone from work. Ever."

"Dating?"

Her cheeks flushed a pale pink, but there was no other sign she was flustered. That wasn't particular surprising. Rachel Browne was tough where it counted, and didn't let much get under her skin. Guy wondered if she had equal access to her softer side.

"Fine, *dating* wasn't the right word. Getting involved."

"Where does friendship fit in?"

Her lips, painted her famous red, curved up at the edges, although he wasn't sure if she was amused by his comment or just stalling for time. "In case you haven't noticed, Guy, I'm pretty used to keeping my own counsel, as it were."

He didn't laugh, even though he wanted to. She was so serious, so reserved—just shy of standoffish.

A powerful image of Rachel standing in her doorway, wearing that incredibly see-through red nightie almost made him choke on his meat loaf. Shit, was all this interest in Rachel simply because he'd seen the shape of her breasts? The way her nipples looked so dark and tempting beneath the silk? How her slender waist made him want to run his hands down the curves of her hips?

No, even he wasn't quite that shallow. Almost. But not quite. It was what had happened after that that had prompted his interest. When they'd talked. When she'd opened her closed emotional door that little bit. "You're right," he said. "You have every reason not to go with me. I was insensitive to ask. I'll be fine."

She didn't exactly frown, but her eyebrows came down just enough for two little indents to bridge the top of her nose. It made him want to take back his noble, but totally insincere words. Then she reached down beside her chair to get her purse. Once it was snugly over her shoulder, she stood and lifted her tray. "Guy?"

"Yes?" He looked up, wishing once again she'd wear her hair down. God, he wanted to see it loose and free.

"What time do you want to leave?"

"Pardon me?"

"I said I was debating. Not that I'd decided."

"And now you have?"

She nodded, and if he had to guess, it was more to reassure herself than him. "I have. As long as you're sure I won't be missed here."

"That's all taken care of."

After a big breath, she smiled. Tightly, but he wasn't going to quibble. "Wonderful."

"I figure we'll be gone three days at the most. Probably two."

"Good, good."

"So why don't we leave tomorrow about six?"

"In the morning?"

"The funeral is at 9:00 a.m."

"Ah. Okay, I'll be ready."

He stood up, his chair loud in the strangely quiet room. "It's not going to be the easiest trip in the world."

"I'm sure it won't be. But we'll do everything we can to find DiGrasso. It seems from what Richie said that Stan's embedded in the community. He makes his living selling drugs, which makes it difficult to relocate."

"God, I hope so. I'm going to find that son of a bitch. It'll be easier if he's not ten thousand miles away."

"Well," she said, "I'd better be on my way. Six will be here before we know it."

He almost put his hand on her arm, but stopped himself in the nick of time. He didn't want to scare her off. "Thanks, Rachel. I'll see you in the morning."

"Great," she said. With that, she turned and went to the side of the room, put her tray on the trolley and walked out, her sensible heels clicking across the tile.

Guy went back to his dinner, although nothing appealed any longer except the pie. He dug into it, wishing it could have been a little fresher. Rachel was going with him to Los Angeles. He couldn't decide if he was more grateful he'd have her by his side at the funeral, or that she was going to help him find Stan.

Regardless, he had to make sure he respected her wishes, no matter what. Separate rooms. Complete discretion. He'd be nothing if not a perfect gentleman.

But maybe, if he was very lucky, he'd get to see the other side of Rachel. The woman behind the stethoscope. And maybe, just maybe, she'd let her hair down.

IT TOOK RACHEL four hours to pack for three days. Every outfit was debated, tried on, discarded. Of course, some of them had been retrieved, folded and put in her suitcase, but she wished like hell there was a twenty-four-hour mall nearby.

Why it mattered what she took, she had no idea. She felt sure, in her saner moments, that Guy couldn't have cared less about her clothes. The only thing she felt the least bit happy about was the black dress she'd wear to the funeral. It was reserved, respectful, and she liked how she felt in it. As for the rest, what did a person wear to apprehend a fugitive? A dress? Slacks?

She ended up with work clothes. Two blazers, a cashmere sweater, three blouses, a skirt and two pairs of slacks. Once she'd decided on the clothes, she picked out the accessories.

At eleven-thirty, she decided what she really needed was a mud mask. Then nothing would do but a bath. Finally, just before 1:00 a.m., she gave up. There was nothing more to keep her busy, nothing to keep her mind off the situation she'd gotten herself into.

Damn that Allie. What had she been thinking? Of all people, she should know that this was not Rachel's forte. Helping out a pal? Being there for emotional support? Please.

Rachel was the cold fish of Courage Bay, didn't Guy know that? Didn't he see that she was absolutely horrible at the whole human-interaction thing except on a superficial level?

No. She wasn't going to go there, not again. She was taking a step outside her comfort zone. People did it all the time, and their worlds didn't fall apart.

She sat down on the edge of her bed. She was going to be driving for hours with Guy at the wheel. Just the two of them. Thank God they could talk shop. That would take up a whole lot of time. And then there was the whole Stan situation. Maybe if she played her cards right, she wouldn't have to say anything personal.

Oh, Lord, he'd need her at the funeral. Really need her. He loved Heather, and was clearly devastated by her death. Rachel couldn't possibly turn her back or even step away. Whatever his emotional state, she'd have to be right there to pick up the pieces. Say the right thing.

Only, she didn't know the right thing to say. She never had.

She flopped back, her hair flying about the duvet, her arms spread like wings. This was such a huge mistake. What on earth had she been thinking?

She'd have to tell him she couldn't go. She'd get up,

make some excuse… She could say she was coming down with a virus. That would work. He'd believe her, and even if he didn't, so what? He wouldn't fire her because she backed out. Then things could go back to normal. The way she liked.

Being alone. Eating by herself. Coming home to a dark house. Spending the weekends trying to fill the hours until she could go back to work.

Rolling over on the bed, Rachel cupped her chin in her hands. "Some wonderful life you've got there, Rachel. Every woman's dream come true."

But no one was there to smile at her sarcasm. To understand the pain that was slightly below the surface.

Whatever she was going to do, she had to get some sleep first. Sitting up, she closed her suitcase and put it on the floor. Then she crawled between her wonderful sheets, fluffing her pillows until they were just so. Only then did she turn off the bedside lamp.

In the darkened room, a sliver of moonlight sneaked between her curtains to illuminate the corner of her dresser. No big deal. It wasn't enough to keep her awake, especially at this hour. All she had to do was close her eyes, and she'd be asleep in no time.

Fifteen minutes later, she got up, rearranged the drapes and crawled back in bed. It was totally dark. Totally right.

And she was so sad, she wanted to cry.

GUY WASN'T SURE she would really go the distance until her suitcase was in the back of the SUV, and she was seat-belted beside him. From the look of her, he was pretty certain he hadn't been the only one with major doubts. But the point was, she was here, and they were off to Los Angeles.

Him and Rachel Browne. Who'd have thunk it, as one of the E.R. nurses liked to put it. He headed toward the freeway, southbound. "How about some coffee for the road?" he asked.

She turned to look at him for a moment. "Sure, that would be great." Then she went back to staring out the front window.

He wondered if it was going to be like this the whole drive down. They'd get to the funeral park in plenty of time, even if there was a lot of traffic on those L.A. freeways. He wasn't looking forward to the end of the trip, and he'd hoped for some distraction on the way.

But maybe Rachel was tired. Probably needed coffee as badly as he did. He spotted a fast-food joint and swung in. "This okay?"

"Fine."

At the window, he ordered for them both. Rachel turned down his offer of food to go with their coffee. It took all of seven minutes, and they were on the road again. But it was too damn quiet. Music? No, not yet. That would be a last resort. He'd let her enjoy her coffee for a few minutes, then he'd start the ball rolling.

He glanced at her, getting a perfect view of her profile. That strong, straight nose, her pouty lips—which, he saw, were painted casual pink, not hospital red. Her beautiful dark mane was pulled back into a tidy bun, neat and proper, and damn if he didn't want to rip out every bobby pin and run his hands through her hair until she looked like a wild woman.

She gasped as he swerved in his lane, not enough to get them into trouble, but enough to force his attention back to the road instead of the woman. He checked, but neither of them had spilled anything. "Sorry," he said.

"That's all right."

"How'd you sleep last night?"

She looked at him, another quickie, before she stared back at the road. "Fine. You?"

"Not so great. Mostly, I was worried about Heath."

"Oh, I didn't even ask," she said, this time turning toward him. "How is he?"

"Holding his own. But if he doesn't improve in a few days, he's going to need a kidney transplant. Another reason to find Stan."

"You think he'd be willing to donate?"

"We'd only need a small section. But then, if he's the carrier of the genetic traits, the transplant might not work at all. The bottom line is, we need DiGrasso for tests, if nothing else. If he can't do it, I'll find someone. I just wish to God I had the right blood type."

"Let's not borrow trouble. You don't know that Heath will even need the operation yet."

"That's true. I just want all my bases covered."

"With Burns as team leader, I can guarantee you that every avenue is being pursued. He's nothing if not meticulous."

"Yeah. I know. But it's not the same as taking care of things myself."

"What you're doing today is important to Heath. You

know that. Not only are you paying your respects to his mother, you're finding his history. It may not be a very nice one, but it's his, and he needs to know what he's up against. Who else but you would do that?"

Now it was his turn to look at Rachel. Not for long, of course; he had no desire to run into a truck. Still, he couldn't help but stare. In her own terribly logical, Mr. Spock-like way, she'd said exactly what he needed to hear. "Hey," he said. "You like music?"

She eyed him warily. "What type?"

"How about country?"

Her eyes widened in alarm.

"Just kidding," he said, hoping she wouldn't open his CD rack and see that he wasn't in the least. "Eagles?"

Her head tilted to the side. "Okay."

"Wait. Classical?"

"Depends."

"On?"

"Mahler in the morning? Not a good thing."

He laughed. "Okay, Mahler's out. How about jazz?"

"Better."

"Grusin?"

"Oh."

That was an encouraging sound. "Aha. Dave Grusin. Excellent choice, Doctor. Here, hold the wheel."

She yelped, but her hand grabbed the steering wheel while he flipped open his CD rack. He found the perfect tape in a second, popped it in the player, then relieved her of her duties.

He felt her staring at him, and he knew for a fact that

if he were to look at her side of the car, he'd see her openmouthed in surprise. "What?"

"You let go."

"But you were right here."

"How do you know I can drive from the passenger seat?"

"You can do an appendectomy with one eye closed."

"Which has nothing to do with it."

"Sure it does."

She didn't say anything as "Mountain Dance" filled the car, the piano flying as high as the hazy winter clouds. When he finally gave in and looked over at her, she was staring at the road once more. But damn if there wasn't a hint of a smile. A tiny hint, but it was there.

Things were looking up.

CHAPTER THIRTEEN

THE COOL OF THE MORNING had just started to ease now that the sun had come out from behind the clouds. Forest Lawn was quiet, except for the birds. The perfectly manicured lawns spread in all directions, interrupted only by grave markers and the occasional statue. It was a beautiful spot for such a tragic ending.

The service itself was graveside, with a minister attending. Only a few people, including Tammy, Heather's father, Walter, and Tammy's elderly aunt, stood beside the casket. Rachel wondered where Heather's friends were. Despite the circumstance of their meeting, Rachel had seen that Heather was a lovely girl, and from her diary it was clear she was bright and could be witty. Had her relationship with Stan isolated her from all her friends?

How had she even met that vile man? He was clearly older than her by at least ten years, and from what Rachel could determine, he was nothing more than criminal scum. But something about him must have captivated Heather, must have fit into her dreams. Was it just the freedom of being away from her parents? Had she been so unhappy in her life that she was willing to go to hell to escape?

As the minister spoke in a southern-accented mono-tone, Rachel's gaze settled on Tammy. She stood sepa-rate from both of her ex-husbands and even her aunt. Her arms were held tightly against her sides, her fingers clutching several tissues that were wet with her tears. She'd dressed with meticulous attention to detail. Her simple dress, dark gray, was on the short side for the oc-casion; her shoes, with their slim heels, were the same shade as the dress, although the pumps were muddied from walking across the grounds. Her mohair coat was an even darker gray that pulled the whole outfit to-gether. A simple strand of pearls around her neck, matching pearl studs and her wedding ring completed the ensemble. Her blond hair had been pulled back in a loose chignon, and her makeup was elegant and perfect. Despite the tears, there wasn't a smudge.

Rachel could see what had attracted Guy. Tammy was a beautiful woman and there was something vibrant about her that grief couldn't hide. What was more a mystery was what Tammy had seen in her first hus-band, Walter.

He was a husky man, balding, and not nearly as well put together as his ex. In fact, there was a stain on his blue tie, and his navy suit was ill-fitting, the sleeves bar-ing far too much of his cuffs. Even his shoes were old, unpolished. Rachel could see he was deeply upset, and the doctor in her worried about his coloring. It was clear he suffered from high blood pressure and didn't take care of himself.

She realized that Walter was staring at her and she averted her gaze, embarrassed to have been caught. She tried to listen to the minister, but the words were so generic it was painful.

Guy hadn't looked at anything but his stepdaughter's casket since they'd arrived. His grief was so tangible it filled Rachel with an awful sadness. She knew he was mourning not only the loss of his stepdaughter, but also what he perceived as his failures. He hadn't been there for Heather, had given her only a small part of himself when he'd had the opportunity to give so much more.

She also knew he exaggerated his sins, that Heather had been grateful to him as someone who had loved her. Guy might not have been his ideal of a father, but he'd been just that to Heather.

Rachel stepped closer to him. Not touching close, but near enough that if he wanted to, he could find her hand. What she wanted was to give him comfort, but she had no idea how.

For so many years she had avoided just such a situation. Without her role as a doctor to protect her, she felt like a child, inexperienced and naive. Which was absurd. She was almost thirty years old, for God's sake. What was wrong with her that she couldn't step away from her own ego to help this man who so desperately needed her?

Feeling ridiculous, she put aside her own discomfort and touched his hand. He gripped her back with such intensity that it hurt. Not so much physical pain as regret that she'd left him alone for so long.

Emboldened, she moved closer to his side. His eyes red-rimmed, he looked at her with such gratitude she felt like the most selfish person on earth. She smiled, and he managed a weak grin back before he turned to listen to the rest of the service.

She concentrated on the feel of his hand. The strength of him. She'd watched him work magic with those hands, healing impossible cases, pulling people from the brink of death. She was struck that despite how helpless he must be feeling now, there was still such firmness in his grip, such confidence.

As the minister began to recite the Lord's Prayer, Guy leaned to his right, pressing against her shoulder. He was a big man, and she doubted she could support his whole weight, but that's not what he asked of her. He simply made contact. One sorry person to another. A touch. A hand. A shoulder to lean on.

Tears formed, and for once she didn't try to blink them away. She let herself feel. For Heather, for Heath, and most especially for Guy.

THE RIDE TO THE HOTEL was silent, and Guy did everything he could to erase from his mind the sight of Heather's casket as it was lowered into the ground. So much wasted potential. A life snuffed out like a tossed match. It was more than he could bear, and Heather wasn't even his biological child.

But he'd loved her. In his own pathetic way, she was the closest he'd ever gotten to having a daughter. He didn't think the opportunity would come again. Perhaps, if he was lucky, Tammy would allow him to be part of Heath's life, but then she was going back to France. From what she'd said, she had no reason to return to America again.

He started when he felt Rachel's soft touch on his arm. "Are you all right?"

He nodded. "We're almost there. We'll get you settled in before we call the hospital."

"Do you think we should let Richie know we're here?"

"Good idea." He smiled at her, touched by the concern he saw on her face. Especially because he knew how hard this must be for her. "You'll have to be the solo brains today, kiddo. I'm not exactly at my best."

"Don't worry about it," she said softly. "Let's just take it one step at a time. First, the hotel. Then maybe something to eat and a rest. We can plan our moves later."

"Not too much later. We've got three hospitals to see."

"Maybe we don't have to go to all three," she said. "I'm sure Richie will help any way he can."

He pulled off the 101 freeway at Wilshire and slowed down to accommodate the downtown traffic. It was two-thirty, and it felt as if every street was crammed with drivers. Bad ones.

"I haven't been to L.A. in a long time," she said.

"You went to school here, right?"

She nodded. "UCLA. But I didn't come downtown often."

"Did you live in Westwood?"

"Most of the time I lived at the dorms. Then, when I did my residency, I shared a house in Santa Monica with four others."

"That must have been a dream."

"It wasn't so bad. We hardly saw each other, and I had a private room. It was an attic really, but it was all mine. When I wasn't studying, I was sleeping, and I didn't do much of that."

"Don't I remember."

"What about you?"

"I went to Harvard. I had an apartment for most of my residency."

"Alone?"

"Nope. But I only shared it with one person."

"How nice."

"Scholarships. And my father's good planning. Didn't your folks help?"

"Not really," Rachel said. "I got a scholarship, too, but it wasn't enough to cover my living expenses. And my dad was in the military. He wasn't exactly rolling in it. They did what they could."

"Where are they now?"

"Living in Mississippi. Biloxi. They're retired, playing a lot of bingo."

"You don't sound close."

"We're not. We were never an Ozzie and Harriet-type family."

"Brothers, sisters?" Guy asked.

"Nope, just me."

"And a lot of moving?"

"We didn't stay in one place too long. Although I was lucky—I got through most of high school in California. Los Alamitos, actually."

"Nice area."

"Near the base. But yeah, it was."

He saw the hotel blocks away. The three round glass towers were the most recognizable of the cityscape.

When he reached Figueroa, he turned into the underground parking lot of the Bonaventure. It took them a few minutes to find the bellman, but soon they were following their luggage to the opulent front desk, their footsteps swallowed by the thick carpet and the sound of water from the atrium. Guy took care of both rooms, making sure they had a connecting door.

The bellhop took them up to the tenth floor, and to Rachel's room first. It was nice and roomy, with a great view of the mountains. There were two queen beds with white cotton spreads, a writing desk and ergonomic chair, and a large bathroom.

She reached for her wallet to tip the young man, but Guy beat her to it. "This is my party," he said.

"I can take care of my expenses."

"I know. But you won't. Now get yourself settled. What do you say I come by in an hour? We'll grab something to eat then."

"Great. Do you want me to call Richie?"

"I'll take care of it, thanks." He looked at her, standing in front of the floor-to-ceiling window, her face in shadow but her concern for him palpable. He didn't want to leave, not now, not tonight, but a deal was a deal, and he wasn't about to rock the boat, not when she was giving so much.

So with a parting smile, he followed the bellman to the room next door. His room was almost identical to Rachel's except he had one king bed. It didn't take him long to get unpacked, since he hadn't brought that much with him. He walked to their connecting doors and undid the lock, but decided not to knock. She might be sleeping, and he didn't want to interrupt. Knowing she was so close made it difficult, though. Just being with her soothed him inexplicably. He pulled out his cell phone, called Richie, and left a voice mail.

Sitting on the edge of the bed, Guy took in the view out the window. Buildings towered over the city, and momentarily he missed Courage Bay. Weariness swamped him, making his shoulders sag and his head loll to his chest. Even slipping off his shoes seemed too much.

So he didn't. He just lay back and closed his eyes.

"GUY?"

He turned, smiling at the soft silk of her voice. How incredible that she was here, naked and so willing. That her lips were so soft and pink and lush—

"Guy, wake up."

He blinked, the light painful and intrusive. He didn't know where he was except that Rachel was there, and she wasn't naked.

"Guy, it's late. If we want to get to the hospital, we'd better get moving."

He was wide awake now, and shocked that Rachel really was in his room, the dream still lingering too vividly.

"I knocked. You didn't answer, so I let myself in," she said, pointing at their connecting doors. "Your phone wasn't working, so you have to call the front desk. Evidently, someone put a block order on it, and only you can get it taken off."

"A block order?"

"I'm guessing it was the last guest. Anyway, I was hungry, and I figured you would be, too, so I, uh…" She pointed to a room-service cart with several domed dishes just this side of the desk.

"Great. Thank you. Give me a minute to wash up."

She walked over to the small dining table while he went into the roomy bath. The wash helped. So did getting fresh clothes from the closet and changing. He checked himself in the mirror, satisfied that his sport coat, blue silk shirt and slacks would look official enough to get the hospital personnel to cooperate.

In the bedroom, Rachel had already started eating. She blushed prettily, and he was so attracted to her at that moment that he nearly made a fool of himself.

Instead he sat down across from her, grateful for the napkin on his lap, and looked at the assortment of goodies she'd had brought in. There was shrimp cocktail, a crab Louie, a BLT, and a heaping plate of fries, along with a pot of coffee and two cups. "Perfect," he said, taking a large shrimp.

"What about Richie?"

"I left a message." He excused himself and called the front desk. They lifted the phone ban, and sure enough there was a message from Montgomery. Guy got his cell phone and called the lieutenant back. After filling his friend in, Guy decided to go to the most likely hospital, Los Angeles General, where two of the children with Noonan's had been registered. Richie would follow through with the others, getting any information about Stan he could.

The thought of action improved his spirits and he rejoined Rachel at the small table.

"I heard most of that," she said. "Is the hospital far?"

"No, actually, it's just a few miles." He checked his watch, surprised that it was almost six. He'd slept far longer than he'd intended. "We'll have to battle traffic, but I'd like to get there before the shift change."

"Great." She finished one half of the sandwich while he concentrated on the other. They didn't speak, but the silence was comfortable. He used the time to watch her. She'd changed into dark slacks and a pale green blouse, the soft material caressing her breasts, giving him a hint of what lay beneath. Again, he remembered her nightie, and he wondered if she'd brought it with her.

"I was surprised about Walter," she said, breaking into his less-than-noble thoughts.

"Why?"

"Tammy seems like she'd go for someone a little more dashing."

"I imagine Walter had his dashing days. He's met with a lot of failure. That'll take the dash out of any man."

The corners of her lips turned down. "I know."

"Thinking of someone in particular?"

"Yes, actually. I'm reminded of my father."

"He was in the military?"

"He signed up at seventeen. Spent his whole life following orders, but he never really went anywhere. He was a perfect soldier, but was never promoted. He made it to captain. Over the years, it beat him down. He'd never been a happy man, but he became…seriously depressed."

"That must have been hard for you."

"Not as hard as it was on my mother. She's much older than her years now. She hides in her bingo and her vodka."

"Was your father another reason you went into medicine?"

"No. He wanted me to be a man when I grew up."

Guy laughed, although he could see it was no joke. "You blew it. Big time."

Rachel smiled as she lowered her lashes. She was so very much a woman that Guy could barely think of anything else. He couldn't take his eyes off her, not while he finished eating, not through his second cup of coffee.

She was the one who stood first, and when she did, her blouse tightened across her chest. What had been a hint before came out in stunning relief. Her nipples, hard and jutting, were clearly defined.

Guy was at her side before he could stop himself, and she was in his arms. His gaze met hers, asking silent permission. When her lips parted, when her skin glowed with a rosy flush, when he felt her chest rise and fall against his, he bent down and captured her mouth in a kiss that had beckoned since morning.

CHAPTER FOURTEEN

RACHEL TENSED as Guy wrapped his arms around her, his big hands flat on her back, pulling her close against him. She remembered his taste, his scent, and the tension slipped away.

When she parted her lips, he took advantage, his tongue exploring tenderly. The taste of him was stronger now, intoxicating. With a little shock she realized her hand had found the back of his head, and her fingers gripped his soft, dark hair.

He turned, breaking the kiss long enough for her to take in a deep breath of air, to grasp exactly what she was doing. They were in his hotel room, the bed a few feet away, his body pressed against hers so she could feel the hardness of his chest, the edge of his belt buckle, the thickness of his erection against her hip.

At the moment of revelation there were no lightning bolts, except perhaps the one inside her, the one that flashed when she thrust her hips closer, brought her hand to his shoulder to keep him right there.

He moaned as he ran his hands down the length of her back, as his tongue teased and explored, and she thought for a moment of Allie, of how proud she'd be that Rachel hadn't run for the hills.

God, it had been so long, too long, since she'd been touched like this. That hint of a kiss in his office had set off some kind of change in her, etched away at the numbness she'd felt for so long. And now it was as if she'd been awakened in all her private places. His touch, his kiss, the awareness of his hard body...

He pulled back, his eyes dilated and hungry, his lips still moist from where she'd licked him. "Oh, Christ."

She nodded.

"I hate this, but we have to—"

"I know—the time."

"The time."

Rachel stepped back, her face as heated as the rest of her. One part of her was amused by her own embarrassment, while the other part felt triumphant. She'd kissed him, and she'd only freaked a tiny bit. Not enough for him to notice. Not enough to spoil the deliciousness of it all. "I'll go get my coat and purse."

"Great," he said, his chest still rising and falling too quickly. "I'll put the dishes outside."

She headed for her room, stopping in the bathroom to fix her hair and lipstick. She decided to put on her fire-engine red, her work lipstick, but when they finished with their business tonight, she'd take it off. Maybe that wouldn't be the only thing she took off.

Grabbing her coat from the hanger, she slipped it on slowly. Guy was still her boss. So why wasn't that thought so troublesome anymore?

THE FAMILIAR SMELL of the hospital calmed Guy as he escorted Rachel to the administration office. There they would meet Estelle Potter, who, Montgomery had assured him, had already pulled the files they would need.

The offices they passed reminded Guy of the Courage Bay administrative suite, although these weren't as nicely decorated.

Ms. Potter sat behind a neat metal desk, dotted with pictures of what he assumed were her grandchildren. She reminded him a bit of his aunt Dianna, white hair cropped short and stylishly, her dress a pale blue, her smile welcoming.

"Please, sit down, Doctors," she said. "Lieutenant Montgomery told me what you were looking for, and I hope I can help." She reached behind to a long credenza and picked up three manila files, then handed them to Guy. "These three infants had Noonan's. All of them were born within the last five years. Unfortunately, none of them survived. It was a tragedy, really. There was no prenatal care at all, and two of the mothers were addicts."

Guy looked at Rachel, his stomach constricting at the tragic outcomes in the files. The M.O. sounded very familiar, and at least that gave him some hope of finding the man behind all this.

He handed one of the files to Rachel and opened the top one on the desk.

"Can I get you some coffee?" Ms. Potter said. "It's not bad."

"We'd love some, thank you," Rachel said. "I like mine with cream and sugar, Guy prefers his black."

"I'll be right back," Ms. Potter said. "You take your time."

Guy didn't even hear her leave, he was so busy reading the file. The first thing he looked at was the birth parents. The father's name was Stan Olivetti. Stan. There was an address in Hollywood, but it was from well over four years ago. Regardless, he pulled his notebook out of his breast pocket and jotted down the name and address. Then he read the medical report.

The child was born to a crack-addicted mother. He'd had severe Noonan's and had, of course, been born addicted. He'd lived for eighteen hours, all of them spent in the NICU. The mother had disappeared a day after giving birth. There had been no follow-up care.

"The father here is Stan Taylor," Rachel said, her voice low, as if they were in a library.

"What address?"

"Tarzana."

Guy swore. He was hoping there would be one area to comb, but Tarzana was in the San Fernando Valley, thirty miles away. He handed her the pad. "Could you note it, please?"

She nodded, absently taking the pen and pad, her gaze still on the file. "The infant was born addicted," she said. "Which isn't true about Heath."

"But the rest is."

She sighed. "Yes. Except that Heath isn't as severely compromised as this child."

Guy thanked God for that, then opened the second file. "Stan Taylor again," he said. And this time the address was back in Hollywood. It wasn't the same location as the first file, but it was closer than the Valley.

"Here," Rachel said, handing him back his pad.

He jotted down the address, marveling at her clear

handwriting above his. "How did you get to be a doctor?" he asked.

She looked at him quizzically.

"I can read your writing."

Her smile made everything better. His mind went right back to his hotel room, to the feel of her in his arms. She was so warm and lush, it had taken all his strength to pull away from her.

Ms. Potter walked back into the room holding two mugs. She put them on the desk, then walked around to her seat. "Anything?"

Guy nodded. "Yes. We think all these children had the same father, using assumed names."

"We can't do much about that," she said. "We don't ask for identification unless there's insurance involved."

"Of course not," Rachel said. "But at least we have two addresses in the same area. That's something."

"Maybe the lieutenant will find out more," Ms. Potter said. "I wish I could have been more helpful. So tell me, you're from Courage Bay? I knew a nurse that moved up there about two years ago. Her name was Carol Stone."

Rachel smiled, and as Guy reread the files on the desk, the women talked about their mutual acquaintance. Thankfully, they didn't ask him to participate. What he wanted was to get out of here and check out the Hollywood addresses.

When he closed the last file, Rachel put down her coffee mug and stood up. Reaching across the table, she shook hands with the administrator. Guy did the same, thanking her for letting them keep the files; they were duplicates.

It wasn't until eight-fifteen that they got to the first Hollywood address. It was on Argyle, and the neighborhood was just what Guy expected it to be. Dingy apartments, drug dealers and hookers on the corner by the public phone. The address Stan had written down turned out to be a liquor store, single story. A complete dead end. They didn't have a photo of Stan, or even a vague description, but Guy couldn't just give up.

He also couldn't leave Rachel in the car, so they went inside the liquor store. The man behind the crowded counter could have used a bath. He also needed to peel his eyes off Rachel before Guy lunged over the cash register.

"Do you know a man named Stan?" Rachel asked, her back straight, her voice like steel.

"Just Stan?" the clerk asked, showing yellowed teeth. "Oh, yeah, he was just here. Bought some candy."

"Enough, smart-ass," Guy said, pulling out his wallet. He peeled off a twenty and threw it on the counter. "His name is Stan, and he has a habit of getting young women pregnant."

The clerk grabbed the twenty as if it was springloaded. Then he smiled again, at Rachel. "I know a lot of pregnant chicks."

Guy took a step forward, but stopped when he felt Rachel's hand on his arm.

"Let's go," she said softly.

He wanted more from the idiot behind the counter, but Guy could see it was futile. He let Rachel lead him back out to the cool night air and the car. Just in time. The crowd around the phone had taken notice of his SUV.

Once Rachel and he were inside and the locks engaged, Guy drove slowly, heading toward the second address. It was close by, only about six blocks.

"Guy, are you sure we shouldn't just go? Ask Richie to check it out?"

"How about I drop you off at the hotel?"

She shook her head. "No, let's go."

He reached over and took her hand. Her skin was cold and yet the touch warmed him. She warmed him.

They checked his Thomas Guide map and arrived at yet another depressed area, but this time, it was an apartment complex instead of a store. The address had listed 2A, but Guy didn't hold up much hope that Stan would be waiting there.

They parked under a streetlight a half block from the entrance. He walked around to open Rachel's door, but she was already on the street. It felt so natural to put his arm around her shoulder, to feel her hand slip to his waist. It was as if they'd been doing this forever, walking together, touching.

But he was also acutely aware that this was time out of his normal life. That she was here because he'd practically begged her, that she was reacting to the unusual circumstances. What he wanted was for this to last, for the closeness he felt to stay with them when they were back in Courage Bay.

They walked up a short concrete path to a building that was crumbling. A twisted metal door hung on a loose hinge. Above that were the remnants of a security camera. "Crack house," he said. "But I think its heyday is over, or we'd never be able to get in."

As it was, they walked past the flimsy door into a shadowed hallway. Offensive smells wafted from the peeling walls, and only one overhead light worked.

They found the staircase in the middle of the hallway, past silent closed doors. He wondered if anyone lived in the building anymore, but then he heard a shout from above. Halfway up the stairs, he heard a dog bark, a baby cry.

Rachel had taken his hand, and he held her tight as they arrived on the second floor. Across from them, the apartment door was open, and looking inside, he saw several filthy mattresses on a cluttered floor. They found 2A and knocked on the door. There was no answer.

Guy tried the knob, and it opened with a squeal. He wasn't sure if it was safer to leave Rachel outside or take her with him, but the way she gripped his hand, he doubted he'd have a say. He took a step, then two, his eyes slowly adjusting to the dark.

More mattresses, a broken television set on a cardboard box. Trash littered the floor like a carpet, and the smell of urine was strong and fetid.

"Did you hear that?" Rachel whispered.

He hadn't, but he stilled and listened. A moment later, he thought he heard a moan coming from somewhere behind a door in the rear of the apartment.

"There," Rachel said. "Come on." She pulled him forward as they stepped gingerly over the detritus of who knew how many junkies. She knocked on the door. "Hello? Are you all right?"

The response was another moan.

Rachel opened the door. Inside, a single lightbulb illuminated a room in slightly better condition than the one they had passed. There were only two mattresses in here, and a dresser with one drawer missing. Huddled in a shadow at the back of one of the beds was a girl.

ALL RACHEL COULD really see were wide, terrified eyes. Those eyes closed as the girl clutched her stomach and moaned in pain. Rachel turned to Guy. "Call 911," she said, then she let go of his hand and walked to the bed. "What's wrong?" she asked, keeping her voice soft and low.

"It hurts," the girl cried, sounding no older than a teenager. She leaned back so Rachel could see her swollen belly.

"Oh, God," Rachel whispered. "Guy, she's pregnant." Rachel sat down, touched the young girl's forehead. She was clammy but not feverish. "Are you alone here?"

The girl's hair was plastered to her scalp, and her arms were so thin that Rachel wondered when she'd last eaten. "They left."

"Who left?"

"Every—" The word cracked as she buckled with another spasm.

"The ambulance is on the way," he said.

"Help me," Rachel said, then turned back to the girl. "How far along are you?"

"I don't know. Five months, I think."

"Can you tell me about the contractions?"

The girl looked at her as if she was crazy. "I'm not having the baby," she said.

"You're not having contractions?"

"No. I just need some money."

Rachel got it. The girl wasn't in labor, she was in withdrawal. "We need to get you to a hospital."

"No!" The girl tried to shove her away, but her arm didn't reach far enough. "Just go away if you're not going to help."

"We are going to help. We'll get you to a hospital."

"I won't go. You can't make me."

Rachel didn't argue. "Honey, where's the father?"

She turned her head. "He left."

"Who?"

"What do you care?" She doubled over again, groaning.

"We're trying to find a man named Stan."

The girl shook her head.

"Is he the father?"

"No."

"But you know him?"

The girl looked up at her with pleading eyes. "Give me some money and I'll tell you."

Rachel doubted they'd get any real information from the girl, but Guy already had his wallet out. It wouldn't do any harm at this point, since there was no way they were leaving her here to get more drugs. At the hospital, the doctors would try to save the baby, get the girl in detox.

The teenager grabbed the twenty from Guy's fingers and gripped it in her clenched fist.

"What can you tell us about Stan?"

"I only know one guy named Stan. He used to live here, but he moved."

"Did he have a pregnant girlfriend?"

She nodded. "He wanted to give away the baby. To that adoption lady."

Rachel looked at Guy, then back to the bed. "Do you know her name?"

The girl shrugged. "Ann somebody. I don't know."

A siren sounded beyond the closed window, but the girl didn't seem to notice.

"Do you remember Stan's girlfriend's name?"

"I don't know."

"Are you sure?" Guy said, holding out another twenty.

The pregnant girl grabbed the second bill. "Heather, I think. But she's gone."

Guy put his hand on Rachel's shoulder. "Heather," he whispered.

The siren stopped and Guy went to guide the paramedics to the bedroom. Rachel stayed, grateful that this child would get some help. If she remained in the hospital long enough, it might make a difference in her baby's life. But with crack addicts, that wasn't very likely to happen.

The paramedics took over as soon as they walked in. Guy pulled Rachel to the side. "I called Richie. Told him about the adoption angle. He's going to get on it."

Rachel rested against him, comforted by his strong arm around her shoulder. The girl, who still wouldn't give her name, struggled with the paramedics, not wanting to go, but it was clear they'd handled this kind of situation many times before. They gave her a mild sedative and finally got her on the gurney. She cussed at the

EMTs, at Guy and Rachel and at someone named Eli the whole way out of the apartment and down the stairs.

Guy talked to one of the paramedics after the girl was on board. Rachel looked up to see a small crowd standing across the street. They were mostly kids, some looking bored, some anxious. She wondered how many of them called that squalid apartment home.

So much hopelessness. So much pain. But Rachel had realized long ago that all she could do was help the patient in front of her, do her best to keep on task, because if she let the pain in, she'd be useless.

She looked at Guy, knowing he'd go to the ends of the earth to find Stan and stop him from harming any more innocents. She understood. But his determination, his obsession, scared her.

The ambulance doors slammed shut, and Guy came back to her side. "Let's get out of here," he said.

They walked the half block to their car, and as he opened her door, he touched her arm. Then leaning over, he lowered his lips to hers.

The kiss was gentle, comfortable. He touched her cheek with his cool fingers. "Thank you," he said softly.

"For what?"

"For being here."

She smiled sadly. "Her odds aren't very good."

"Better than if we'd never found her."

She leaned against the car door. "Do you think that was his plan? To sell the babies?"

Guy dropped his hand, closed his eyes. "It's possible. Although if the children are all so sick…"

"But they probably wouldn't all have Noonan's."

"No. Some of them might have been all right."

"Maybe that's why he got so many of the girls pregnant—to increase his chances."

"Hell of a way to make money."

She shuddered. "He needs to be stopped."

"He will be."

Rachel stood up again, and this time, she kissed Guy. "You're doing a good thing," she said.

"*We're* doing a good thing."

CHAPTER FIFTEEN

IT WAS TEN-THIRTY by the time they made it back to the hotel, and Rachel was exhausted. Guy didn't look all that chipper, either, but she could also feel an undercurrent of tension in him. Tomorrow, they'd continue the search for Stan DiGrasso, and they'd follow through on the adoption angle. But to do a good job, they both needed to sleep. It seemed days ago that they had stood by Heather's grave, but Rachel knew that once Guy relaxed, he'd be filled with the memories. "What do you say we go get a drink?" she suggested.

"Sure. There's a bar on the first floor that looked quiet."

He got his claim ticket from the valet, and they headed to the elevator. Another couple waited with them. They were older, in their sixties, Rachel guessed, and they stood in companionable silence. Just as the elevator opened, the man, dressed in a dark suit and coat, took his wife's hand. She smiled at him with such warmth, it made Rachel move closer to Guy. How long had that couple been together? Years and years, she mused. Sharing all the minutia of life, the breakfast dishes, the laundry. They didn't speak at all on the ride up, but they were together in a way Rachel barely understood.

At the main lobby, Guy took her hand as they walked to the bar. Touching him like this didn't have that kind of comfort. She hardly knew the feel of his skin, the strength in his hands. And she found herself wanting to. Wishing things could be different. She wished *she* could be different—the kind of woman who could share like that.

It wasn't as if she hadn't tried. But the only men in her life who'd mattered had wanted too much.

They entered a small upscale bar. Soft jazz came from hidden speakers. The bar itself was semicircular and incredibly well stocked. The bartender was a beautiful woman, wearing a crisp white shirt and black bolo tie. Her hair was long and loose, much like Rachel's when she let it down. Three couples sat at separate round tables, and a single man in a business suit perched at the bar itself. Guy chose a table in the farthest, darkest corner, which suited her just fine.

"What can I get you?" he asked after she'd slipped off her coat and sat down.

"A gin and tonic, please."

"Be right back."

He left his coat on an empty chair and headed to get their drinks. She watched him, admiring his long, lean body. He walked with grace and confidence, something she'd recognized in him from the first. This was a man who was used to being in control, and it must be killing him to feel so helpless about Heather, about Heath. It made perfect sense that he had found himself a mission. He was looking for closure and, she suspected, a form of absolution.

The bartender gave him a generous smile, which was also understandable. Guy was a very handsome man.

She thought about kissing him, the way they had this afternoon. He was just as good at that as he was at cooking. Better, maybe. She was a fool for a great kisser, but she hadn't been lucky enough to find many. She wondered if Guy would be just as wonderful in bed.

The thought made her warm, excited. She wanted to sleep with him—there was no point even trying to deny it. Not that she could afford to disregard her concerns, but maybe she could put them on hold for one night.

She knew she'd never be thinking this way if they were back in Courage Bay.

Guy returned with two drinks. He put hers on the table, then sat down. He ran his hand over his face and looked at her with tired eyes. "Quite a day."

She nodded. "A lot for anyone to take in. But I think we made progress."

"I hope so. I've been thinking about the adoption agency. It can't be legitimate if they're getting babies from the likes of DiGrasso."

"That would be to our advantage," she said. "The police would have taken notice."

"That's what I'm counting on."

"I like your friend," she said.

"Richie?"

She nodded.

"He's a good guy. Not that we're that tight. Just sailing buddies. We've shared a few drinks from time to time. If he'd just sent me on my way, I wouldn't have thought twice about it."

"That makes me like him all the more."

"Yeah, me, too."

She sipped her drink, which was cold and perfect. "It feels like three in the morning."

"You, too, huh? I'm exhausted, but I don't think I could sleep to save my life."

"The drink will help."

He looked down at his glass, then back at her. "I'm too worn out to play this with much finesse," he said. "I want to take you upstairs." His gaze searched her, every part of her face. "I want to make love to you."

She felt the flush start from the inside and spread to every part that mattered. It wasn't that the subject was a surprise, just the way he'd brought it up. "Oh," was all she could think to say.

He closed his eyes briefly, then leaned back in his chair. "I won't ask again. I promised not to seduce you." He smiled. "Guess I lied."

"It's okay," she said, not sure whether she was forgiving him for the lie, or agreeing to his proposition. She wanted to make love with him, but now that the offer was there, on the table, her confidence wavered. "May I ask you a question?"

"Of course."

"Why?"

"Why…?"

"Why me? Why now? We've known each other for a couple of years, and you never gave any sign that you were interested in more than a professional relationship."

He sat quite still, looking at her deeply. "I've tried to

figure that out," he said, "but frankly, I haven't come up with a compelling reason."

"But something must have changed."

He nodded slowly. "Something did. When, exactly, I'm not sure. I hate to admit it, but I think it began when I came to your house."

She knew exactly what he was talking about. She'd been so sleepy she'd opened the door half-dressed.

"I'd like to think I'm not so easily swayed by a beautiful woman," he said. "And now that I've questioned my motives, I've come to realize that it may have been the spark, but it wasn't the fire."

"I don't understand."

"I'm not surprised. It's…complicated."

She leaned forward, amazed at his candor. "Go on."

"This isn't easy, but I'll try. I've admired you for a long time. Actually, since the day we met. Part of my decision to hire you was that there was so much more to you than your technical skills."

She thought about what Allie had said. That she was a great technician but had no heart. "But I'm the Iron Lady, don't you know that? Don't you listen to the hospital gossip?"

"I can't escape it. I've heard all that, and I've watched you with a lot of patients. What I saw was that you were tightly controlled. That your clinical approach was a mask for something much deeper. That's what got me." His gaze wandered her face again, more leisurely this time.

She felt very self-conscious, perhaps even more than she had on that awful morning when she'd learned

Heather was his stepdaughter. Now it was as if he were seeing her secrets.

"I want to know what's underneath that rigid control," he said, his voice so low she had to strain to hear. "I think—and it's just a theory, mind you—but I think there's a deep and burning fire somewhere inside you. That what you show to me, to the hospital, to the patients, is a whole lot of bluff. That you, my dear Iron Lady, are a maelstrom of emotions, and that you care so much it scares the hell out of you."

Rachel pulled back, her heart beating so hard she could barely breathe. Never in her life had she felt so exposed. So vulnerable. She couldn't stand it, not for another second. She stood, grabbed her coat, her purse. "I'm sorry, but I have to go. Just call me when you want to leave in the morning."

She took a step away, not wanting to look back, but she had to. His face, shocked, worried, filled her with excuses, none of them acceptable. She did what she'd wanted to do since the moment he'd opened up to her. She fled.

GUY FINALLY TURNED OFF his light at a quarter to twelve. He was so damn tired, and so torn up about what he'd said to Rachel.

He'd clearly hit a chord, but he'd had no clue that it would cause such a reaction. If he'd been more discreet, more careful, she wouldn't have run. He was a fool, and he had no excuse other than his bone-deep weariness. His impatience with anything less than the truth when it came to himself had bled where it didn't belong. Just because he was faced with some brutal facts about his own life was no reason to go probing in someone else's.

He tried to get comfortable, but the pillows weren't his. He threw one to the side of the bed and punched the other until he'd created the perfect cushion.

Closing his eyes, he welcomed the idea of sleep, but that's not what he got. Instead, the morning crept back in vivid images. The sound of the birds in the trees. The stain on Walter's tie. The drone of the minister and his sterile words. But mostly what came to him was the coffin. The box, so benign by itself, held a lifetime of love and joy and pain and discovery. And was stealing a future that would never unfold.

Heather had deserved so much more. She'd deserved parents who weren't emotional cripples. A stepfather who wasn't so consumed with his own life that he couldn't see two feet in front of him. She'd deserved a healthy baby, a loving husband and a world of possibilities, instead of the nightmare her life and death had become.

He threw the covers back and turned on the light. Sliding his feet into his slippers, he got up, found the remote control and turned on the news.

It was sports coverage, but he didn't care. He wanted the voices. When his restlessness wasn't appeased, he walked to the honor bar. The scotch he'd had at the bar earlier had done nothing, but maybe wine would do the trick. He wished he had something more substantial to put him to sleep, but he so rarely needed help that he'd never thought to bring anything with him.

He unscrewed the wine bottle, which wasn't actually

a bad Merlot, and poured it into the tumbler next to the ice bucket.

Then he sat in the chair by the desk, turning his seat so he could see the television. But his gaze didn't go there; it went to the connecting doors.

Maybe she was awake. Maybe he could talk to her, apologize. He was not sorry for what he'd said, but how he'd said it. And when. The relationship was too new and raw for revelations, especially with someone like Rachel.

Everything about her was closed and tight. The way she wore her hair, her tailored clothes, the way she held her body. Maybe that's why the sight of her in the wisp of silk had shocked him into seeing her in an incredibly new way.

The hell of it was, he couldn't go back. Never again would he look at her as the prim celibate. The all-work-no-play trauma doctor. He'd seen beyond her masquerade, stripped her of her defenses, and now he knew, for certain, that he was right about her.

If she'd laughed at him, changed the subject, touched his hand with hers, he would have doubted. But her reaction had been electric, as if he'd given her three hundred joules with the defibrillator. The look on her face had been outrage, and that's what troubled him most. She wasn't just shocked he'd guessed her secret, but wounded.

Just as he'd been wounded when he'd realized exactly who the hell he was. Truth was a bitch.

RACHEL TURNED OFF the television. She wasn't watching it and the ads annoyed her with their perky messages and perfect people. She sat cross-legged on the bed, readjusting the pillows behind her back.

She couldn't stop thinking about what a moron she'd been downstairs. The man had made a few guesses, that's all. Thought he knew her when he really didn't. They worked together, that's all. They'd barely spent any time together, and she'd certainly never bared her soul to him. Not the way he'd done to her.

She'd never asked him to expose himself like that. In fact, she really didn't want to know anything about his personal demons. The hell with what Allie had said, she wasn't involved, and if she could just keep her wits about her, she wouldn't be involved. She'd seen a man in pain and offered a helping hand. Period, the end. Hell, his pain had nothing to do with her. Nothing.

Of course she felt badly, she wasn't a monster. He'd lost someone important to him. But where was his sister during all this turmoil? His brother? He was the one with the family, not her. It wasn't fair.

She flung the covers back and stood up, wishing she had her own car. It was probably too late to rent one, and she wasn't about to ask Guy for his keys. But maybe there was something open downstairs. This was L.A., for heaven's sake—of course there'd be something happening. She could go back to the bar. Have a few drinks. Get sloshed.

By the time she reached the wardrobe, she remembered she didn't like to get drunk. And why? Because she was a control freak, that's why.

Okay, so he knew that about her. Big whopping deal. Everyone knew that about her. Hence her nickname. It wasn't a crime. It was sensible, especially for a physician. If she wasn't in control, everything would go to hell. Who would help the patients? They were the only ones who mattered.

Deep and burning fire inside her, indeed. What was he, some kind of psychic?

Projecting. That's what he was doing. Projecting his own neurosis on her. He was the one who had all that stupid fire, not her.

This was ridiculous. It was late, and she had to get to sleep. A bath. That would calm her down, get her to relax. She went into the bathroom and started the tub.

While the water flowed, she brushed her hair and pulled it up on top of her head. Then she dug into her train case and got out an oatmeal mask, plastering her face with it so she looked like a Kabuki dancer.

Then she pulled out her cuticle cream and lathered that on her fingers. When she checked behind her, the tub was filled enough for her to get in.

Stripping off her long nightgown, she hung it on the back of the door. Then she tested the water with her toe, adjusted the taps and stepped in.

She felt better immediately. The steam, the warmth were a balm to her troubled nerves, and she smiled for the first time since she'd run from Guy.

It took her a while, but she lay all the way down, the water coming almost up to her chin. She closed her eyes, resting her head on the tile behind her.

No permanent damage had been done. She felt sure that Guy would back off now, that they could get through tomorrow focused on finding Stan and the adoption agency. No heartfelt talks, no baring of souls. She would just be Rachel, and he would just be Guy.

Sexy, handsome Guy.

She shifted, feeling a warmth that wasn't entirely from the water. Damn, if only…

If he'd just kept his mouth shut, who knew what might have happened. She still wasn't averse to the idea of sex. In fact, she rather liked the thought of it, especially with the man in question. With those big hands and the way he kissed.

Sighing, she cupped some water in her hand and let it dribble over her breast. Her nipple hardened into a tight bud. It wasn't nearly enough.

Her hand moved down over her belly, sliding across her wet skin, resting just above the nest of dark curls. She shivered, anticipating. If anything would help her relax, this would.

Good old self-gratification. The one sexual relationship that would end up exactly as she wanted it to. No muss, certainly no fuss. She could trust herself not to say anything foolish.

Although, clearly, she couldn't stop herself from thinking very foolish thoughts.

She pictured herself getting out of the tub, putting on her bathrobe and walking to the connecting doors.

It wasn't a leap from there to imagine him opening the door, tousled from sleep, wearing only pajama bottoms. They'd be riding so low on his hips she could see the line of dark hair below his belly button. He'd smile, say nothing. Just step back, inviting her in.

Because this was her fantasy, she wouldn't speak, either. She'd simply walk to the side of his bed, and with slow, deliberate movements, open the robe. Watch his eyes as he realized that she had nothing whatsoever underneath.

She'd let the robe drop at her feet, and he'd notice her toes were painted. That her legs were smooth.

In her mind's eye he walked slowly toward her, his eyes dark and smoky, his body delicious with all those muscles and hard parts.

Her eyes opened and the dream dissipated. Suddenly the old standby wasn't what she wanted at all.

She sat up so quickly, the water sloshed on the tile floor, but she didn't care. Quickly, she washed her face, scrubbed the goop off her hands and climbed out of the tub. Wrapping a towel around her, she patted herself dry.

The plan had been so simple. Nothing to it. She'd pleasured herself a hundred times before.

Impatiently, she ripped the pins out of her hair and flipped the whole mess behind her back, then she marched out of the bathroom, picked her robe up from the side of her bed and slipped it on.

Walking over to the connecting doors, she knocked. Three times. Loudly.

CHAPTER SIXTEEN

HE WAS DREAMING. He had to be, because if he wasn't, Rachel wouldn't be standing in the doorway, wearing a bathrobe, and she definitely wouldn't be looking at him with that naked hunger in her eyes.

"You were sleeping— I'll go," she said, stepping back.

"No! I mean, it's fine. Come in. In fact, I wasn't sleeping." He was the one to step back now, letting her into his room. His gaze caught on her hair. It wasn't in a ponytail or up in a bun. It was loose and flowing, silky smooth and more beautiful than he'd imagined. His fingers itched to touch it, to touch her.

He closed the connecting doors, and by the time he turned around, she was standing by his bed. Even in the dim light of the bedside lamp, he could see her cheeks were flushed with color, and her hands were on the belt of her white terry robe. She wore no shoes, and her toes—my God, they were painted a deep scarlet. Guy didn't know what to look at. Her toes, her hair, her incredibly moist lips, luscious and full. She decided for him when she untied the knot of her belt.

He tore his gaze from the open belt to her face,

making damn sure he understood what was happening. As soon as their eyes met, he knew without a doubt.

Standing so still he could practically hear his own heartbeat, he waited, holding his breath.

She ran her slender hands up the center of the robe until she grasped the ends. Slowly, teasingly, she pulled the robe open, revealing the treasure beneath.

His throat tightened and he felt himself harden as he drank in her beauty. She was the most stunning woman he'd ever seen, and he felt humbled just to be able to look at her. Her skin glowed. Her breasts, so perfect they begged to be caressed; her nipples, dark like wine, taut and dimpled.

He let his gaze wander lower, lingering over the indent of her waist, the flat of her belly, the curve of her hips. His mouth opened when he looked at the trim triangle of dark hair barely hiding her womanhood. And how her thighs, lovely and strong, tapered to her knees and shapely calves.

He should do something. Move. Speak. But he couldn't. She was so much more… The combination of brains, skill and beauty overwhelmed him. He'd never felt such need. Every part of him wanted every part of her. He had no explanation, just gratitude.

The robe dropped to the floor, leaving her utterly naked. Gorgeous. Then she moved her right hand slowly up the side of her body until her fingertips touched the peak of her nipple.

He closed the distance between them in three strides, and she was in his arms, her breasts pressed against his naked chest, her gasp swallowed when his lips crushed hers.

GUY'S MOUTH ON HERS took Rachel by surprise, bringing her to the dizzying realization that she was here, with him. That she'd come to him naked and willing. That she'd stripped herself bare before him. And then the amazement was all about the way his hands were on her body, running over her chilled flesh, warming her all the way through. The way he took possession of her mouth, his tongue thrusting and darting, leaving no part of her untouched.

She parried with him, tasted him, teased him while she explored the contours of his back. He'd been half-naked, just as she'd imagined. Instead of pajama bottoms, he'd worn sweats, riding low. No shirt, just muscles, heat. Power.

He pressed against her and she felt his excitement, and not just from the hard thickness against her hip. It was in the thrust of his tongue, the pressure of his fingers.

She'd done it. She'd thrown away every sane thought she'd ever had and come to him. She wanted to laugh at how bizarre it was, but he kept her occupied. He leaned back, but only for a moment, taking a great breath of air, and then he kissed her again, hard. His lips moved to her cheek, the curve of her jaw. Little nips that felt almost like pain, and then his tongue, licking her like a cat. She felt his lips at the hollow of her throat, kisses, tiny kisses, below her ear, and then her earlobe between his teeth, making her shiver and squeal like a child.

His laughter...she could feel it in her chest, her hands,

her hips. Just before his mouth found hers again, he sighed, and her breath and his melded, mixed, became the same.

This was exactly where she wanted to be. With Guy. This night. In this tall tower with the lights glittering outside like diamonds.

His hands shifted, moving her closer to the bed. A moment of struggle, then abandon as she let herself fall with a whoosh onto the mattress, her head sinking into the pillow.

Guy next to her, his fingertips gently smoothing the strands of hair from her forehead, her cheek. Then he was gone, and she turned her head to watch his fingers curl under the band of his sweats. He pulled them down over his erection, and she was embarrassed that her mouth fell open.

He was so beautiful. Strong, lean, powerful. Dark hair on his chest, then tanned skin over muscle. A fabulous discovery that he was an innie, with a neat little belly button that seemed so innocent until her gaze moved down.

"Oh, God," she said, not intentionally. She'd seen hundreds, maybe thousands of naked male bodies, but this... He made her insides tighten, her breasts crave his touch.

This was a totally new experience, as if it was her first time with a man. Nothing had ever felt like this. She laughed.

She wasn't Rachel anymore. Not the same Rachel. He made her someone different. Someone who wanted to touch every part of his body, to have him inside her.

Naked now, and shimmering in the faint light, he climbed on the bed. She moved with the weight of him, rocked with his movements. She expected his kiss, but he was too far away. At the foot of the bed.

She raised her head higher, until her neck ached, but he wasn't looking back. He lifted her foot, cradled it in his hand. Kissed her right there. The tender, ticklish arch.

She tried to pull away, but he held her steady, smiled down at her, then turned his attention back to her foot. It was incredible and weird, and she wasn't sure what he was going to do, so she ignored his teasing and focused on his body.

He was sitting back on his knees, his legs underneath him so that his thick length rested on his thigh. His masculinity, his power made her dizzy, and she gave up, letting her head fall back to the pillow.

She jerked up again a second later when, to her shock, Guy licked the bottom of her foot, then swallowed her big toe. Gasping, she struggled. She'd never— "Guy!"

He didn't even look at her. His tongue was too busy licking. Sucking.

Her strength waned, her head fell back again, and sensation swamped her. The hot, wet warmth of his mouth, the slickness of his tongue. It dawned on her that this was what it must feel like for a man to be in a woman. Not nearly as good, because the toe didn't have a tenth of the nerve endings of the penis, and yet…

She moaned. He was sucking her toe and she couldn't stop her own sounds of pleasure or her head from tossing from side to side. He was killing her, and she didn't know what to do with the feelings that weren't just in her toe, but all the way up, inside, making her wet and hot and ready.

As if he realized she couldn't take it for another second, he let her go. Well, not entirely. His hands moved up her leg, followed by his lips. He nibbled on the back of her knee, yet again making her feel so strange, so wonderful.

Quieting herself, she could hear his breathing, hard, fast, heavy. Kissing her in all these strange places was giving him pleasure, too. But it wasn't enough. It wasn't what she'd come for.

She pulled her leg free and got up on her own knees, grabbed his shoulders in her hands and yanked his mouth to hers. He kissed her again as she ran her hands down his chest, tweaking his nipples between her fingers, loving his response, his low groan. Her hands moved farther down, his skin amazingly thin and smooth above the hard steel of muscle below. So different from her own softness. And still it wasn't enough. She slid her hands down and grasped his hard length.

He gasped, and at that second she darted her tongue inside his mouth, invading him and thrusting, letting him know exactly what she wanted him to do to her. She guided her hands up the length of him, over the smooth head, and spread his moisture as she traced the corded muscle on the underside.

His tongue pushed back, battling her for domination, and she gave him his way. But only for a moment. Before he could guess her intentions, she put her hands flat on his chest, astonished that she could feel his beating heart, that his rhythm matched her own.

She pushed him, hard, and he fell flat on his back,

his legs bent beneath him. She allowed him to straighten them, then straddled him quickly, using her hands and her upper-body strength to hold him down.

Staring down at him, she saw the wild hunger in his eyes, and the thought that she was seconds away from having him made her want to scream in triumph. Never letting up on her hold, she lifted her lower body and planted her feet on the bed, next to his hips. She leaned down until her lips almost touched the shell of his ear. "Hold yourself," she whispered.

She waited, keeping still until she felt his hand move. Then the tip of his length teased her entrance. He was ready, and she was nearly out of her mind with want.

Slowly, as slowly as she could, she lowered herself, inch by astonishing inch. Her stomach tightened, and she was unable to breathe.

He stretched her, filled her, and still she squeezed her muscles, knowing he could feel every move. He closed his eyes and his muscles jumped beneath her hands.

She lowered herself even farther until she rested completely on his body. Her head lolled back as she gasped for breath, more aware than she'd ever been in her life.

And then she began a slow rise, lifting herself, the only connection between them her hands on his chest, and the heat of him inside her.

She continued, straining, moving so slowly, and then his hands gripped her arms, tightly. The next second, she was thrown from his body, tossed on her back on the bed.

He was the one on top now, holding her firmly down. She pushed against him but she couldn't move. "Hey," she said, wanting him back inside her. It was his expression that made her still.

"Wait," he said, his voice low, as steely as his muscles. "Don't you move. Not a muscle."

She couldn't look away, couldn't avoid the intensity of his gaze. Finally, with no choice, she nodded.

He relaxed his hold and swung his right leg over so he was beside her. Taking a deep breath, he ran his hand through his hair, which formed into sharp spikes from his sweat. He got off the bed, and her disappointment turned to understanding as he grabbed his case off the desk and pulled out several foil-wrapped packages.

She felt like a fool. Of all people, she should know better than to make love without protection. Didn't she warn her patients about that time and again? She'd lost it, that's all.

Lost it.

It had never happened before. She'd never been so carried away that she'd let her survival instincts fail. What was he doing to her?

His weight shifted on the bed, and then his leg was over hers, and just as she'd done to him, he straddled her hips. He didn't touch her, though. Resting on his knees, he was a scant inch above her body. She felt his heat, and she wanted him with a mind that was barely her own.

What he did next made her almost as angry as she was needy. He smiled at her, clearly so pleased with himself he wanted to crow.

"Fine," she said. "You thought of it. I didn't. So gloat if you want."

"I'm not gloating about this," he said, tearing open the packet.

"Then what's that smile for?"

"Because I've got you exactly where I want you."

She started up, pushing her elbows into the bed, but his hands came down, stopping her short. "Let me go," she said, serious as a heart attack.

He shook his head, his smile fading, replaced with something that stirred her from her breasts to her center. "No."

"Guy, let me—"

He cut her off with his lips on hers, a hard kiss, demanding, fighting her. Struggling.

Winning.

She hadn't realized she was pushing against him until she gave up. The war wasn't over, just this battle. Watching him sheath himself, knowing he was teasing her with his unhurried movements, she squirmed, wondering briefly if she was indeed losing.

When he was done, he pushed her legs apart with his knees. Her breathing quickened. His hands held her down, his legs controlled her movements. She was helpless beneath him, and that thought made her crazy, except that she knew exactly what he was going to do to her, and she wanted that as badly as she wanted to move.

Want overpowered will. She closed her eyes and forced herself to relax.

Guy felt her muscles grow lax underneath his hands. Her legs stopped pressing against him. Her chest rose and fell rapidly as she struggled to let herself yield to him.

"That's it, Rachel, let go," he whispered. "Let it all go. All you have to do is relax, let me give you pleasure." He leaned down until his mouth was just above hers, until her breath became his. "Let me make you come."

She gasped, and he kissed her. Impressively. Controlling. That's what this was about. Control, and he wasn't about to let her win. She was his, and he would have her. Tame her.

Release her.

He reached down, guiding himself to the soft folds of her entrance. Pausing there, making her feel his power, he let her anticipation build and climb until he could feel her quiver underneath him. Then he entered her…as slowly as she had ridden him, the torment just as strong.

He wanted to plunge inside her, to hear her scream his name until she grew hoarse. But his desires were secondary to what she truly needed. Abandon. He wanted her to lose her mind, and he wasn't above doing whatever it took to get her there.

When she opened her eyes, he held her steady with his gaze. As long as she continued to see him, he'd give her everything.

He pushed his hips, keeping to the slow, steady, killing pace. She closed her eyes. He stopped.

It took three times for her to understand. When she did, she cursed him, quite succinctly, but her eyes stayed open. And then it truly began. The war was almost over, and the peace would be one neither of them would ever forget.

As he moved faster, he was blown to the moon by the

feeling of being inside her. He was shaking, he could feel it, and as he stared into her eyes, his peripheral vision caught a drop of sweat fall on the edge of her cheek. But he didn't give in, and he didn't stop. Well, he stopped for a while. Reveling in the sensation of being in her. Part of her.

But she was so trusting…

He began a new rhythm, pumping in, out, faster and harder, and then he wasn't the one in the driver's seat anymore as his body took over, guiding him, pushing him.

He felt her heels on his back, her legs squeeze his hips, and he was the one who lost it, who couldn't hold back the cry that came from the middle of his soul. He kept his eyes open through sheer force of will, and Rachel…God, so beautiful…she never closed her eyes, never looked away, just maintained the connection even though he knew her body was wild with the need to explode.

It was close for him now, and nothing on heaven or earth could stop it. He felt the pressure build and build, and at the last possible second, he kissed her, and her mouth was open and she was bucking under him like a woman untamed. Her scream filled him until it became his scream and he was coming so hard he thought he might just die.

CHAPTER SEVENTEEN

RACHEL'S HEART finally slowed down after Guy had curled himself around her. He'd given her water, a pillow, and pulled the covers up over both of them, and then he'd wrapped her in his arms.

His breathing was deep and even, and she suspected that if he wasn't asleep yet, he soon would be. She wanted to sleep, but her thoughts fired so rapidly, she doubted it would happen. The experience of making love with Guy was still too raw.

He'd taken her to a place she'd never known. Forced her to accede to his demands. Despite everything, part of her was still furious—the part of her that wanted control. But giving in had shown her so much. Almost too much.

What he'd said about her at the bar was true. She was terrified of the very thought of losing control, whether it was in the E.R. or the bedroom. Why? What would it cost her to let go of the reins?

Somewhere along the way, she'd come to believe that the loss of control was life or death. That if she let go for even a moment, all would be lost. She'd lose, she'd be weak.

Her father had told her time and again that she could never let anyone get the upper hand. He'd viewed his life as a series of battles, mostly losses, where anyone who had power over him was the villain. Whenever he'd lost a promotion, it was someone else's fault. Someone who had more juice. A bastard who didn't know his ass from a hole in the ground.

God, how often had she heard that? Her mother had always agreed with her father. She'd given him everything. Her heart, her spirit. And on some level, Rachel's father had despised her mother for it.

Maybe that explained it. Knowing that her dad took everything her mom had to give, kept her cowed, under this thumb, but reviled her for those very things, was the underpinnings of her own need. Rachel had been desperate for her father's respect, and the only way she'd ever gotten it was by achievement. He had been fiercely proud of her accomplishments and contemptuous of her failures, so she'd dedicated her life to being the best.

He'd watched her when Molly had gotten sick, and he'd made no bones about the fact that her deep sorrow was a weakness that would be her downfall if she didn't control it.

And she'd believed him. The fear of weakness had guided her every move. It had hardly been a choice. That attitude was so ingrained in her that she'd never considered an alternative.

Of course, she'd seen other people who didn't live their lives as she did, and part of her had categorized them all as somewhat pathetic. Except for Allie.

Allie was the exception, perhaps because Rachel had

been witness to her happiness. Yes, Allie was successful, but her career was only a part of her life. She loved her friends, her family. She had outside interests, like music and dancing and her obsession with film noir. With Allie, compassion came first, everything else second.

Not that Rachel could become like her friend, but perhaps it wasn't too late to have a broader view of the world.

When she'd let go in Guy's arms, there had been a sense of freedom she'd never experienced in her life. To know that he would take the lead, that she was safe letting him guide her, that he wouldn't hurt her... Even thinking those thoughts felt foreign and somehow bad. As if she were disappointing her father, whom she didn't even admire.

Who was to say that she couldn't make a new choice? That she couldn't learn to ease up, to let someone else win? To relax and appreciate the people in her life, instead of just seeing where they fit in her personal hierarchy.

She touched Guy's hand where it lay over her shoulder. Felt his warm breath on the back of her neck and his body pressed against hers. A wave of gratitude hit her so profoundly that tears fell from her closed eyes.

He was still her boss. There was no way they could have a relationship within the confines of the hospital. But this night, this awakening would be with her forever. If she let it. If she didn't go back to the status quo.

The whole idea of change scared her. Especially a change so fundamental. But now that she'd gotten this glimpse of an alternative to the way she lived, it would be too uncomfortable to do nothing.

She just wasn't sure she was strong enough.

RICHIE MONTGOMERY LOOKED just the same as he had the last time Guy had seen him. Medium height, dark, thinning hair, a beer belly that attested to his fondness for a good ol' time. But his country-bumpkin appearance deceived many a luckless criminal. Richie was smart and thorough, and very little escaped his keen eye. Guy was pleased he was on board and that his determination to find Stan DiGrasso almost equaled Guy's own.

"Come on back to my office," Richie said, shouldering Guy aside to take Rachel's arm. "If I'd known you were so pretty, I'd have kept you on the phone a lot longer."

Rachel smiled and let Richie lead her into the small office at the back of the North Hollywood police station. He sat her down in one of the two wooden captain's chairs, then went around to his own black leather chair behind the desk.

The top of his desk was neat, considering the amount of paperwork on the file cabinets, the in- and out-boxes, the bookcase on his right. And there were pictures, too, of his wife, his three kids, mostly taken on his sloop.

Guy sat down, his muscles reminding him of the night before. Not that he had been able to think of much else. My God, it had been—

"So I got some interesting information from a friend of mine," Richie said, leaning back and folding his arms over his ample stomach. "Seems there was an adoption agency running out of Hollywood, near the Gower Gulch, that was closed down by the feds about a year ago. It was a sting operation, and the owners, Frank and Ellen Yoder, got out of Dodge before the indictments went through. They're wanted for child selling, falsifying documents and child endangerment. A lot of the children they placed ended up having severe health problems that weren't disclosed, and then there was the way they got their clients." He shook his head. "It wasn't pretty, I can tell you that. A whole mess of heartache from top to bottom, and no convictions."

"The FBI has no idea where they went?" Guy asked.

"Not a clue. But they did find mentions of your Stan DiGrasso—mostly checks. There were a few addresses on him, but he wasn't at any of them. The closest they got was last year, when an informant placed him in Tarzana."

"We found that address," Guy said. "In the files from L.A. General."

"He's not there now. But the man makes most of his money from dealing. Crack, heroin, meth, all kinds of goodies. That's our best hope now. I've talked to some folks in Vice, and let's just say there isn't a cop in the county who hasn't got an eye peeled out for this bastard, excuse my French, Rachel."

"No problem, Lieutenant. It's wonderful that you've done so much."

"Not a problem. We all want this joker caught and put behind bars."

"Is there anything else we can do today?" Guy asked. "We've got a few hours before we head back to Courage Bay."

"Not a damn thing that I can think of. I wish there was. I know it's easier when there's something concrete to work on. Best thing I can think of is for you to get back to that baby. Make sure he's okay."

"I spoke to his doctor this morning," Guy said.

"Heath's doing better. His kidney is functioning well, which was the biggest worry."

"That's great news. How about you let me take you out to a great little steak house I know. It's just around the corner, and they have the best damn cherry pie you've ever tasted."

Rachel gave Guy a look, a tiny nod. He knew she wanted to get home, but saying no to Richie now would have been a slap in the face. "Sounds great."

"All right," Richie said, his Mississippi accent still strong after all the years he'd been away. "We can take my car." He stood up and walked over to Rachel. "And darlin', you're so damn pretty, I think I'll run the siren the whole way."

"MAYBE HEATHER'S DEATH has changed her, too," Rachel said. They were an hour outside Courage Bay, and still talking about Heath and Tammy. She didn't mind, but she wasn't sure she could simply walk back into her life without saying something about last night.

"I don't know. Tammy's priority is still Tammy. I just can't see her dedicating herself to a child with as many issues as Heath has. He's going to be a handful, and she's never been known for her patience."

"Give her a chance, Guy. People can change. I believe that."

He looked at her for a long beat before turning his attention back to the road. "I believe that, too. Funny, I never used to. But now…"

"What?"

He reached over and took her hand in his. "You were amazing last night."

She looked down at their hands, not quite knowing how to react, surprised that she was pleased. "You played me."

"Yes, I suppose I did."

She looked at the highway, up at the darkening sky. "What do you want?" she asked finally.

"I don't know what you mean."

"Yes, you do. You took a huge risk last night. You pressed when you didn't have to. Hell, I made everything very easy."

"Excuse me, Dr. Browne, but there's never been anything easy about you."

"Come on, don't be evasive. You know what I'm talking about."

"Yeah," he said, his voice gentler. "I do. I suppose I had no business, but damn it, Rachel, what I said last night is true. I think you're an amazing woman. I also think you don't give yourself very much slack."

"No, I don't. I never have. It's what's made me a good doctor."

"In part. I agree that discipline is important, and that there's a line that's fuzzy about giving everything to your patients. But it's not all or nothing. At least, it doesn't have to be."

"I have a friend who's always amazed me. She's so balanced with her life, it could be written up in one of those women's magazines. She has friends, a family she loves, a good job. She's funny, she's kind."

"But?"

"But I never understood her. Allie's always been a mystery to me. It was as if we were born on different planets. On mine, there was only winning. Only being the best."

"And on hers?"

"Completely different set of rules. Rules I never figured out."

"But you admire her."

"For a lot of reasons. I just never thought I could be like her."

"And now?"

"I don't know. I hope so. It's daunting."

"I understand more than I care to. This has been a mind-boggling week for me. But then, I've bored you about that enough already."

"Come on. It's obviously true-confessions time. Just talk."

His smile was good. Honest. "I'm not ready to. Not yet. There's still a lot to think about."

"Okay, I won't push you. But I'm here when you're ready."

"I know that, and I appreciate it more than you can imagine. One thing I will say is, I don't expect anything from you." He shook his head. "No, that's a lie. I'm hoping for friendship. If possible, more than that. But I won't push, either, and I won't make it uncomfortable for you at work. It's a tricky situation, and I wouldn't dream of compromising your position. But know this, I'd like to see you."

She slipped her hand from under his. "I don't know, Guy. You're still—"

"Your boss. I know that."

"I don't know what people would say if we were seen dating. It could be a pretty big mess."

Guy nodded. "The pleasures of small-town life."

"Courage Bay isn't a small town."

"The hospital is. And I'm very aware of what your career means to you. Trust me, Rachel. Nothing will happen that you don't want to have happen."

She should have been pleased, but she wasn't. He'd left the ball in her court, which was exactly how she liked to play. But for once, she wished she didn't have to make the decision. Because she knew that despite the night with him, there was nothing more important to her than her career. "Thank you," she said.

He didn't say anything. But she couldn't help but notice how his hands tightened on the wheel. There was nothing to do about it. She couldn't see them pursuing a relationship. Not now, not while they both worked at the same hospital. If there was a chance anyone would think she was with him for political reasons, it could destroy them both.

GUY PICKED UP Heath and held him close to his chest. The boy looked so much better than just two days ago. His color was good, the jaundice had nearly vanished. He was moving more, too, and if Guy hadn't known about his genetic abnormalities, he would have sworn he was a perfect baby boy.

He sat down in the rocker next to the incubator, grateful he could finally dispense with the face mask so he could be close to Heath. What was he thinking? Heath was perfect. And now he had a much better chance of making it, although his health was still vulnerable. But the fact he didn't have to go through a kidney transplant was a damn good sign.

If anything happened to the boy…

Closing his eyes, Guy rocked this child who had no blood connection to him. No connection at all, and Guy had never felt closer to anyone. Except perhaps one person. Just last week he hadn't loved anyone but himself. Hadn't dreamed that he could care like this. Now there were two people who mattered more than his own life.

And he couldn't have either of them.

"Well, that's a picture."

Guy turned to see Tammy standing next to one of the NICU nurses. He hadn't expected her here, especially at this hour. It was only seven-thirty, but for Tammy that was the dinner hour. In fact, she was dressed to go out— in a slinky purple dress and high heels. "When did you get here?" he asked.

"This morning." She came over to him and smiled down at the baby. "He looks better."

"He is. But he's not in the clear."

"So I've heard."

Guy stood and offered the baby to his grandmother. She hesitated, looked down at her dress, then held her arms out. Guy carefully made the transfer, even though a part of him didn't want to. He got another chair and brought it next to the rocker. "Sit," he said, nodding toward the rocker.

Tammy did. Her gaze was on Heath, and even though she smiled at the baby, Guy could see she wasn't relaxed with him. He'd never seen her with an infant before, but he imagined she'd been much like this with Heather. Babies were so helpless, and that was the role Tammy preferred. She simply didn't know how to be the care-giver. He didn't believe it was malicious or even mean-spirited on her part, but it was there, and had been one of the things that had drawn him to her in the first place. He had felt like a big man, taking care of her. He'd been an idiot.

"So what did you find out on your fact-finding mission? Is he in jail?"

"DiGrasso? No. We didn't find him. But we got closer. A lot of people are looking for him now."

"I hope they find him," she said, "but I'm not hold-ing my breath."

"Don't count it out. We made a connection between Stan and an adoption agency. Evidently, he made a habit of impregnating young women, then selling their babies."

That got to her. She stilled, and her face, so perfectly made up, paled. "Oh, God."

Guy leaned forward, resting his elbows on his knees. "We didn't do right by her, Tammy. Neither of us."

"You were hardly there."

"I know. I'm not excusing myself. I could have been so much more. I'm sorry. I didn't know how to be a father."

Tammy's lips were tight together, staring at him, and he could practically see all his sins run through her mind.

"Or," he admitted, "a very good husband."

His ex shifted her attention back to the baby. "I'll find a good doctor for him," she said. "And I've already started to look for an au pair."

"So you've decided to take him?"

"What are you talking about? Of course I'm taking him. He's my grandson."

"But do you want him?"

"Don't start with me, Guy. This isn't your business, and you have no right to judge me. You know nothing about my life. Nothing."

"Why don't you tell me."

She opened her mouth, then closed it again. "What are you trying to pull? You think you can make up for being a shit to Heather by being the perfect father to Heath? I have news for you, buddy. He's not yours. If Heather hadn't come here, you wouldn't have even known about him. I doubt you would have called me, and I'm sure as hell you wouldn't have called Heather. Heath isn't here to make you feel less guilty. You want to be a good father, go have a child."

Guy leaned back, feeling slapped. She was right. He had no business questioning her motives or her decisions. He was, for all intents and purposes, out of the loop. Maybe that's why it was so important for him to find DiGrasso.

But knowing he wasn't wanted or needed didn't make him love Heath any less. The boy had changed him in ways he hardly understood. Losing him would be as devastating as losing Heather.

"You're right," he said. "I'm not his family. But I'd like to be. Somehow."

"Unless you plan to move to France, I don't see how that would be possible. And if you move to France, I'll kill you myself."

He laughed. One thing about Tammy, she'd always made him laugh. But it didn't change the bottom line. He didn't want Heath to go, and he couldn't figure out a way to keep him here. "I don't know, Tammy. I haven't a clue how it would work. Just do me a favor. A big one. Don't shut the door, not yet."

She looked at him, and her expression told him he wasn't making much sense. "I'm leaving as soon as Heath is able to. If you want to see him, I won't stop you."

"That's generous. And I appreciate it." He stood up, ready to leave her to her grandson.

"Guy?"

"Yeah?"

"I don't know what's happened to you since I left. But it's good."

He smiled as he walked away. He didn't even tell her how to put the baby back into the incubator.

It was late, and he hadn't been home yet. He wanted to unpack, get a good night's sleep. Would that be possible? He'd gotten through the day all right, but behind every thought, every bite of food, every blink of his eye was the memory of last night.

To say that it had been extraordinary was a shameful understatement. He'd been with his fair share of women, and had had some fantastic times. Better than he deserved. But last night had made every other experience pale in comparison.

But was it love? Or were his feelings for Rachel some kind of reaction to Heather's death and Heath's condition? Or maybe he was just losing his mind. Nothing had prepared him for the soul-wrenching truths he'd faced in such a short period of time. He was a man who had been given a lot of gifts, which he'd always taken for granted. Things had come easily to him. School, medicine, women, jobs. He'd had few real struggles. Maybe that's why he enjoyed sailing so much. At least there he had a worthy opponent and had to be on his toes.

Since the morning of Heather's death, it was as if the blankets had been thrown off his life. He'd been bared to himself, and what he'd seen upset him more than he could have anticipated.

He got down to the first floor and headed for his office. Connie would be long gone, and he'd have time for himself. If he could get it together, he'd head home, but before then, he'd take a quick look at what had happened here in his absence.

When he turned on the lights, he smiled. There was a plate of chocolate-chip cookies on Connie's desk, covered with plastic wrap. Everything looked as neat and tidy as he expected, even in his office.

Reports were piled on the right corner of his desk, phone messages to the left. But he didn't look at either after settling in his chair. Instead, he closed his eyes and leaned back.

What did he really have in his life? He was happy in his job, although to be brutally frank, he wasn't terribly challenged by it. He'd wanted the power of the position, but he'd given up his work in the trenches. Most of his duties were administrative and while he took on the occasional case, the other doctors did the lion's share.

He had his home. It was nice, but the only place he was truly happy was in the kitchen. Thinking about cooking made him smile. Funny, that was a task he did solo. He never wanted help when he was concocting some new dish. He also liked to sail alone. For such a social guy, that was interesting, no?

Okay, so he had cooking. Being a doctor. Sailing. What he didn't have was a close relationship. Someone with whom to share the real joys of his life. The women he'd dated hadn't tempted him to include them in his private life. Until Rachel.

He'd loved having her in his kitchen. And he'd thought a lot about having her over for more meals, letting her get wild with béarnaise or even a spicy Thai curry.

He'd pictured her a hundred times on his boat. Always with her hair down. Laughing into the wind.

Having gotten a glimpse of Rachel's inner fire, he couldn't imagine not having more. As far as he was concerned, he didn't give one damn what anyone at the hospital thought about the two of them together, but he knew without a doubt that Rachel cared.

She'd never, in his experience, stepped one foot outside the tight restrictions of hospital protocol. Oh, she took chances where a patient's well-being was at stake, but she was a by-the-book attending physician, who made sure her team toed the line at all times.

He'd often wished that she'd participate more in the social aspects of the life here, but that wasn't Rachel. If there was a party, she'd make a brief appearance, then quietly disappear. If someone had a gripe about a co-worker, she was the perfect mediator because she never let her emotions get in the way.

But the woman in bed with him was a wild creature, filled with so much passion it scared her to death.

What an incredible life it would be to watch that part of her blossom. He wanted to be there. To see the whole woman emerge from the tightly woven cocoon she'd created for herself. There was no doubt in his mind that Rachel had already taken the first steps on her journey, and damn it, he wanted front-row seats.

The question then was how? How could he be involved in her life? In Heath's life? How could he salvage a true and meaningful life from the pathetically shallow existence he'd been too blind to see?

CHAPTER EIGHTEEN

HER FIRST DAY BACK was a bitch. There were two frequent fliers, regulars who came in a couple of times a week complaining of this and that, always with a new angle, desperately needing attention. EMTs had brought in a homeless man so dehydrated they almost lost him. Throw in a couple of seekers, drug addicts who came up with amazingly inventive ways to con the docs out of narcotics, and she'd had a full E.R. without any traumas at all. Of course, there had been legitimate patients, too. The flu season was in full throttle, and that meant there were lots of folks moaning in chairs. A broken wrist from a construction site, an impacted bowel and a sprained ankle rounded out the morning. Lots of busy-work, and no time to think. Which was the good part.

The bad part was that whenever she did have a second to herself, all she could focus was Guy. For the second night in a row, he'd kept her awake. Only, it was being without him that had her tossing and turning last night. This was crazy. She couldn't possibly miss him. He was right here at work, so what was her problem?

Maybe it was the whole lack-of-sex thing. Before last night, she hadn't been with a man in over a year. And for a normal, healthy woman, that was just too long a dry spell. Except that she hadn't missed sex at all, until last night.

The memories of what he'd done, what she'd done, and what they'd done together, had her completely unsettled.

She'd actually stayed and listened to Amy's terrible jokes in the lounge. She'd talked for almost twenty minutes to Betty—the patient who'd fallen from her bicycle and sprained her ankle—about her boyfriend. Twenty minutes Rachel could have been catching up on her files, doing rounds, a hundred other things.

She blamed Guy. It was his influence that had sent her heading toward the deep end. Getting back to work this morning had made her realize just how deeply under Guy's spell she'd fallen.

Her life was just fine, thank you very much. And though she loved Allie like a sister, there was no way she could be like her. She didn't even *want* to be like her. Rachel had dedicated her life to one thing—medicine. How could she undermine all that because Guy was great in the sack?

All she wanted was to get back to the way things were. To think of Guy as her boss. Period. Becoming friends with him wasn't going to work.

She thought about telling him right away, but reconsidered. This was private business, and the hospital was such a hotbed of gossip it was too dangerous to have that kind of conversation even in his private office. Still, she really had no choice, and there was no time like the present.

Putting aside her report, Rachel headed for the restroom to check her hair and reapply her lipstick—the dark red that meant all business. Then she walked over to Guy's office.

Connie gave her a big smile. "I've got some fresh cookies, Dr. Browne."

"No, thanks, Connie. But I would like to see Guy."

"Can't help you there." Connie shifted her phone pad and leaned closer to Rachel. "He's up in the boss lady's office. Been up there for over an hour."

"Oh, well, I'm sure he's catching up on the days he missed."

"Right," Connie said, although she didn't sound very convincing. "I'll tell you something that's all hush-hush. You remember that gentleman you worked on the night of the storm? Nepom was his name."

"Yes, I remember. I couldn't do much to help."

"And I'll tell you why. It wasn't the roof that killed him. Someone knocked the stuffing out of him. It's murder."

Rachel sat down. "Murder?"

"That's right. Hit with a hammer at the base of his skull."

"I don't know what to say. There was so much cranial damage."

"I'm not implying that you should have known. Heavens no. But I hear that Callie Baker herself went to the autopsy, and that's where they found it."

"I see. So is that why Guy's with her upstairs?"

Connie leaned back. "I'm not sure. He didn't tell me much. Just let me know he had things to discuss with her."

"You know, I think I'll take you up on one of those cookies."

Guy's secretary smiled and handed her the platter. Rachel took one but barely tasted it. She was too busy thinking about Nepom, and how she hadn't seen the hammer blow.

"Would you like Dr. Giroux to call you when he gets back?"

"Yes, please. I'll be here till about six."

"I'll let him know."

Rachel stood, grabbed one more cookie, then headed back to admitting. If there was no one in chairs, she'd pull the records on Nepom and see what she could see.

GUY RANG RACHEL'S doorbell, then ran a quick hand through his hair. He'd been surprised at her invitation, and pleased when she'd insisted that they have dinner at her house. But most of all he was anxious to tell her about his day. His decision.

She opened the door, and he was struck yet again at how the sight of her knocked him right out. God, she was something. She still had on her slacks and jacket from work, although the lab coat and stethoscope were history. She must have stayed later at the hospital than he'd guessed, because she still wore her power lipstick.

"Come in," she said, opening the door for him.

He entered, then did what he'd wanted to do since dropping her off last night. He touched her cheek, then leaned in for a kiss.

She seemed hesitant, but not for long. Once his arm wrapped around her waist and he pulled her close, she opened her lips to him, and it was L.A. all over again. Scorching heat and a desire that was pure animal swept through him, nearly kicking him on his ass. It was Rachel's hand behind his neck that kept him steady. That, and the promise of what was to come.

She pulled back first, her face flushed. Then she closed the door.

"How do you do that?" he asked as he turned to face her.

"Do what?"

"How come I just kissed the hell out of you and your lipstick is still perfect?"

She smiled. "Magic."

"Ah, that explains it."

"'There are more things on heaven and earth, Horatio…'"

He grinned. "Especially when it comes to women."

She walked past him, heading to her living room. He followed, checking out her place. There was so little of Rachel to be seen. Everything was neatly in place, the decor traditional and comfortable, but it felt more like a model home than the place where someone as vital as Rachel would live. But then Dr. Browne wouldn't have concerned herself much over decorating. She'd have been too busy working.

"Would you like a drink?"

"Love one," he said. "Sorry, I didn't bring any wine, but I was stuck at the hospital until about twenty minutes ago. I wasn't sure if I would spoil dinner if I was late, so…"

"No problem. I have some decent Shiraz, if that's okay?"

He nodded and joined her in the kitchen. She handed

him the corkscrew and the bottle of wine, then went to the oven and peeked inside. Something smelled good.

"I was trying to figure out a way I could make you believe I cooked this," she said, "but it's not gonna happen. I got this from that little Italian place by the hospital. And I bought prepackaged salad with bottled dressing. Sorry."

He poured them each a glass of wine, then joined her by the oven. "I wouldn't have cared if you'd ordered a pizza. I'm not here for the food."

"Right. You gourmands are always jonesing for a store-bought salad."

He gave her the wine. "As a matter of fact, I buy them myself. So shut up and drink."

She eyed him but obeyed. "I heard you were up with Callie Baker today."

Backing up, he leaned against the island. "God bless the grapevine. Yeah, I was."

"I also heard that Bruce Nepom's death was actually a murder."

"I heard that, too, but that's not what I was discussing with Callie."

"Oh."

"I want to tell you about it."

"Okay." She sipped, then jumped. "Dinner. Okay, let's, uh, do this." She opened the fridge and pulled out a big wooden bowl filled with greens. Handing the salad to him, she nodded at the banquette. "Please?"

Guy continued to help until everything was ready, and Rachel had taken her seat across from him. He was nervous, there was no doubt about it. But he was also excited. More excited than he'd been in over twenty years. He couldn't wait to tell her what he'd done, and what he wanted to do.

But he'd also picked up an undercurrent from his beautiful companion. She was a little hectic, unfocused—not her usual M.O. Maybe it was because he was here, on her turf. Or because, like him, she couldn't stop thinking about a repeat of the other night. God, how often he'd thought about that.

"Your plate," she said.

He handed it to her, and she served him a large portion of lasagna. If only he were hungry, this would be a great meal, but the truth was, his stomach was in knots. He had to talk, and do it soon. But first some wine.

"So what did you want to tell me?" she asked.

He put his glass down. "I've made some decisions," he said. "About my life."

"Oh?"

He nodded. "I'm going to keep Heath."

Her fork clattered to her plate. "Excuse me?"

"I'm going to keep him. Raise him. I'm going to do whatever it takes to adopt him as my son."

"But you said Tammy was taking him back to France."

"If I truly believed she'd be happier with him there, I'd send her off with flowers. But I don't. I think she's terrified of Heath, of his health issues. She doesn't want to be a mother again. She's just come into her own as a woman."

"But…"

"It's not a done deal. She has to agree. But I won't

let her say no. I can do so much for that boy. I can give him everything."

"I'm sorry, Guy, but how? You spend more hours at the hospital than I do."

He felt his gut tighten, but it wasn't regret. Not in the least. "Not anymore."

Rachel, on the other hand, looked like she was about to pass out.

"Drink," he said.

She did, taking a good swig. Then she put her glass on the table, and a long minute later looked him in the eye. "You quit?"

"I did. I gave a month's notice. I figure it'll take me some time to get Heath's bedroom together. And for the hospital to find a replacement for me."

"But you love your work."

"I love being a doctor. I haven't done a great deal of that in the last few years."

"So you're going to be a daddy now? Stay home every day? I can't see it."

"I'm not just going to be a daddy. I'll be consulting at Courage Bay. And when Heath's old enough, who knows? I might open a private practice, or even come back to the hospital. But I know that I want to do this. That having a chance to be with Heath, to raise him, is more important to me than any job. I've really had a chance to think things through this last week. So much has happened, but the one thing that's gripped me like a vise is the fact that I'm not the man I want to be.

"I've been a self-centered fool for a long time. Letting it all slide by. Taking the easy way out at every turn. My marriage to Tammy was a perfect example. You want to know how much of myself I put into that union? It wouldn't fill your glass. When it was over, I barely noticed. In fact, I was thankful, because it meant I didn't have to pretend anymore.

"It's not enough. The job—I wanted it for all the wrong reasons, and what I ended up with is paper pushing and budget meetings. That's not why I became a doctor. Even if Tammy won't let me convince her, I'm not going to continue as the chief of the E.R. I've quit no matter what."

"I couldn't be more shocked. I don't even know what to say."

He slid his hand across the table and grasped hers. "Believe me, it's not a whim. I've been hit on the head by a two-by-four. I guess it was the only way I'd listen."

"You didn't say a word about this while we were in L.A."

"I didn't know exactly what I was going to do until last night. I just knew I was going to do something. Set a new course. I've been given a second chance, and I don't want to blow it. Not this time."

"Have you told your family?"

He shook his head. "Only Callie. She was great, by the way. I wanted to tell you next."

The look in her eye scared him. She wasn't getting it. Of course, this new direction in his life would be the last thing she'd ever do.

"How can you know this is the right thing?" she asked.

"I can't. Not for sure. But I haven't felt like this in so long, Rachel. Not since I got my residency. I felt as if I was on top of the world back then. Scared out of my mind, but I was excited about every single day. That's what this is like. I feel years younger. All I want is a chance to watch Heath grow up. To be a real doctor again. To be in charge of my life instead of just going along for the ride."

She sighed, shaking her head. "I'm happy for you. Although, I must admit, it won't be the same in the E.R. You're a wonderful chief, Guy. The best I've ever known."

"Thanks. Really. But I've got a different road now. The E.R. will be just fine without me."

Rachel took another drink, although she didn't think there was enough booze in the house to make sense of all this. She'd known Guy was going through changes, but this was way outside anything she could have imagined.

He was going to give up his whole way of life to raise this baby. And she knew he would give it his best, that no child could be luckier than to have Guy as his father. She had to admire him. It wasn't something she could have done. Not on her best day. "When are you going to talk to Tammy?"

"Tomorrow. I've got to tell you, it's gonna be one hell of a blowout. Tammy can dig her heels in when she wants to."

"Despite the fact that you have everything Heath needs?"

"I don't think it's going to be about Heath. Not at the start, at least. Tammy and I have issues."

"So I've observed."

"I feel badly about that. Most of the issues we have were my fault."

"Oh, now you're just being too generous. Remember, I've met Tammy."

He grinned. "Okay, so Tammy wasn't a complete innocent." His smiled faded. "Heather, on the other hand, was."

"Let's not do that again, okay, Guy? I think you've done enough self-flagellation. We have some really wonderful food here that I didn't cook. Let's eat. And then you can help me with the dishes."

"Sounds great." To illustrate, he dug into the lasagna.

She ate, too, but not because she was hungry. Her head was spinning, and not just about Guy. But about them. If Guy left the hospital, would it change things between them? Did he want to pursue the relationship, or was his dance card full?

Hell, did *she* want to? It hadn't occurred to her that their working together was a safety net for her. And now she felt the need for safety more than ever.

While she wished Guy the best, his abrupt right turn kind of freaked her out. She'd never known anyone to take this big a risk. To turn his back on everything he had and start again.

It scared her. God forbid he wanted her to ride with him. She couldn't. She didn't even know if she wanted her own children, let alone someone else's. It was selfish, she knew, but she simply wasn't ready. It was enough that she was determined to be more open, more caring. Taking on a husband and child was too much.

Heat filled her cheeks as she realized that he hadn't said a word about her in all this. She'd jumped to a pretty damn big conclusion. One that shocked her almost as much as Guy's news.

"What's wrong?"

She cleared her throat. "Nothing."

"Come on, Rachel. Talk to me. We're friends, remember?"

She nodded. "Funny thing about that."

"Go on."

"The reason I asked you over tonight…"

"Was?"

Sitting up straighter, she gripped her glass. "I did some thinking of my own. And while the night we shared together was one I'll never forget, I, uh, don't think it's such a good idea for us to, well…"

"Take it to the next level?"

She nodded. "I'm sorry."

"It won't be an issue anymore. The hospital, I mean. I'll be a free agent."

"I know. What I didn't realize, until we talked, was that the job wasn't what was stopping me. I'm just not ready for a relationship, Guy."

"At least not one with me."

"No. If there was anyone I could be interested in, it's you. Believe that. Like you, I've been hit in the head this week. In fact, I think it was you holding that two-by-four. But I don't work so fast. I'm having a lot of trouble letting any of this in. I don't want to chicken out now. But I can't do it all. I have to take it slowly. To try and be the kinder, gentler me is going to take all the energy

I have. Adding you to the mix? I can't. I don't have whatever it takes to do that."

He nodded, but there wasn't agreement in his eyes. There was hurt, disappointment, and oh, Lord, such pleading. It wasn't fair. He couldn't expect her to be like him. It was enough that she considered him a friend. She couldn't do more than that.

"Guy—"

"It's okay, Rachel. I had no business expecting more. But that didn't seem to stop me from falling in love with you."

She sat back, all the air in her lungs leaving in a whoosh. "You what?"

He gave her a sad little grin. "I know. You probably think I'm certifiable, but as long as I'm on this truth kick, I figure, what the hell? Tell it like it is. I think you're the most amazing woman I've ever met. When all this happened with Heather, it was as if I could suddenly see more clearly. Everything. What I'd done, what I needed to do. And it makes sense that I turned to you in the darkest days. Despite the fact that I barely knew it myself, I've admired you since the day we met. And once I was able to see the real you, the woman behind the red lipstick, I think it was all over. When we were together, it was the most profound experience of my life. That, and seeing my path with Heath… To say it's been earth-shaking is putting it mildly.

"But as I said before, I won't press. You deserve time. All the time in the world. And while I'll miss you, I'll have my hands full. I just hope we can at least be friends…keep in touch."

"I think we can," she said. "But I can't promise. Not yet. I have to see how it goes. How I go." She stood and walked over to Guy's side of the banquette. "Scoot over."

He did, and she slipped in next to him, and then she took his hand. It felt wonderful. Warm and large and safe. "I love what you see in me, Guy. I'm just not sure it's real. I have a lot of thinking to do. You've had an incredible impact on my life—more than any man, ever. Being with you made me feel more alive than any time I can remember. But I have to find me before I can be there for you. For anyone."

He leaned over and kissed her, so gently it broke her heart. "I didn't want it to be this way, but I guess I already knew. That's why I recommended to Callie that you take over as E.R. chief. I know she's strongly considering you, and I hope you go for it. They couldn't do better."

"You did?"

He nodded. "The woman I see is still a doctor, Rachel. I'd never dream of asking you to give that up. Never. It's so much a part of who you are. All I'm saying is that there's more to you than just being a doctor. You're an amazing creature. You have so much to give, and not just to your patients. I want you to be happy, Rachel. The kind of happy that comes from being loved. And loving someone else with all your heart."

She felt her throat tighten with emotion, something that seemed to happen a lot when she was around this man. Now it was her turn to kiss him. And when she touched her lips to his, she knew she wasn't ready to say goodbye just yet. Not quite yet. "Stay with me tonight?" she whispered.

His hands came up to caress the sides of her face. "Yes," he said. "God, yes."

CHAPTER NINETEEN

HE WOULD BE the first man she'd let into her Egyptian-cotton sheets. Maybe this was a mistake, and it would make parting more difficult, but there wasn't a choice. Knowing that they would never be together like this again, sure that in a month, she'd rarely even see him, she needed a bittersweet goodbye to the man who'd changed her life.

Guy stood at the foot of her bed. Her gaze moved down his cream silk shirt, his dark slacks, then back up to the desire in his eyes. The ease with which she'd invited him to her bedroom changed to vague tension, which made her turn off the bedside lamp. The full moon's presence filled the room with a silvery glow, but she didn't feel half so vulnerable. Still, the way her body responded to just the look of Guy was disconcerting. And even more so when he closed the distance between them, when she could feel his heat.

"What's wrong?"

His voice was a whisper, his concern tangible.

"I'm not sure."

"You know you don't have to be afraid of me."

"It's not you."

His lips curled in a wry grin. "Tell you what…" He reached over and cupped her cheek in his warm hand. "We'll do it your way tonight. No tests, no points to be made. Just…" He leaned the short distance between them and kissed her. "Just a sweet goodbye."

She kissed him back, warming to his touch as his hands moved down to her neck. He began to unbutton her blouse, and when her chest was exposed, he bent and kissed the skin he'd revealed. His fingers continued down the blouse until he could pull it back completely.

His lips traced the edge of her bra, then down to her lace-covered nipple. His warm breath made her tighten. Then she felt his hands, both of them, behind her back, and a second later, her bra was undone.

She took care of the rest by taking off her blouse, letting her bra fall from her shoulders, revealing her flesh, her puckered nubs.

As he lowered his head again, she stopped him with her hands on his shoulders. Then it was her turn to work the buttons of his shirt, to strip him to the waist.

He pulled her into his arms, skin against skin. He kissed her hair, hugged her tight, rocked her from side to side. "Rachel," he whispered.

Her hands ran down his back, and she let her fingers play along his muscles. All the tension had left her, and now, in the protection of his grasp, she felt safe, warm, silly for her fear.

When he pulled back, she finished undressing, watching him as he did the same. Leaving their clothes in a puddle on the carpet, he took her hand and led her under the covers.

Nothing was rushed. There wasn't the same urgency that had ruled in the hotel. This was about comfort, and about remembering.

She wanted to touch every part of him, taste him everywhere. She wanted to relive this night in her dreams. She wanted…

"Make love to me," she said, urging him to lie above her. "Make love to me until I fall asleep."

He looked at her, his eyes hazy in the faint light. But she knew he would. Gently, passionately. Marking her forever.

TAMMY CAME TO HIS OFFICE a half hour late. She was dressed in jeans, dark and tight, with a blouse that was so snug it didn't button over her breasts. That didn't seem to be a problem, since the bra she wore matched the red of the blouse exactly.

She tossed her purse on one of his guest chairs and sat in the other. "What's up? I have a dinner engagement in an hour, so if we could do this quickly?"

Now that she was here, he wished he'd had more time to prepare. The day had been crammed with staff coming to see him, making sure he hadn't lost his mind. According to Connie, the memo announcing his resignation had hit the hospital like a bombshell. Of course, he'd talked to his sister, Natalie, before everyone else, and he'd called Alec in Cabo. His family, as he'd known, was supportive, if leery. They'd be nuts not to be. But they stood behind his decision.

Connie was the most difficult to deal with. They'd been together a long time, and she started crying from the word go. But she promised that this month wouldn't end their relationship. She'd come help with Heath when she could, and she'd never let him be without her baking.

"I'm not sure how to do this, Tammy, other than to come right out with it."

Her eyes widened, and he definitely had her attention.

"I'd like to keep Heath here, with me. I'd like to adopt him. Raise him as my son."

Tammy didn't say anything. Her mouth moved a little, but no words came out. She just stared at him as if he'd announced he was moving to Mars.

"I'm sure you're thinking that I have no business raising a child, but I've changed a great deal since we were together. Changed since Heather's death. I'm leaving the hospital. Even if we can't make this work, I've decided to go. I can be at home for Heath. He's going to need a lot of care as he gets older. He'll have heart problems, his kidneys need to be watched. In fact, with Noonan's, there are a host of things that could go wrong, and I want to be there to make sure he has everything he needs. Every chance to have a normal, happy upbringing."

Tammy laughed. Incredulously. It wasn't the reaction he'd hoped for. "Are you insane?"

"I don't think so."

"You want to be a full-time father? You? Who's going to watch him when you're out on your boat, Guy? And what about the women you sleep with? You think they'll stick around when you have a baby in the other room? Not likely."

"As I said, I'm not that man anymore."

"You're not. What, you went to Lourdes? Had a vision?"

"Something like that."

"He's not your grandson."

"I know. But I want him to be mine. I love him, Tammy, more than I've ever loved anyone."

"Including me."

He nodded.

"Well, at least you're honest."

"For once, I'm trying to be. Honest with you and myself. I'm not anything like the man I want to be, and I have a chance to do something about it. The hospital has agreed that I'll be a paid consultant, and eventually, when Heath is old enough, I'm thinking of starting a private practice. But my priority is the boy. His health. His education. His happiness."

"And what do you think my priority is?"

"I think it's exactly the same as mine. Heath's well-being."

She stared at him, then her gaze moved to the window. He noticed she had a car key in her hand, and she worried it, just as she had toyed with the tissue when she'd first come to see him. But he wouldn't rush her. It was a lot to take in. A lot to accept.

"How do I know," she said finally, "that in a week, you won't get bored."

"You don't. All I can do is tell you I've never wanted anything more than this. Anything."

"More than your boat?"

He nodded. "More than my life."

She turned to him again and for the first time, he really saw her age. She was so masterful with makeup that she always looked beautiful, but now he saw she wasn't the girl he'd married. Life had changed her, too. "What about me?"

"You're his family. You'll always be his family."

"I don't have the money to fly back and forth."

"I do. I'll bring him to France as soon as he's old enough, and if you want to see him before then, you can count on me to take care of that. You and your husband."

She shook her head, and his heart lurched. "I don't know, Guy. I've just gotten used to the idea of taking him home."

"I don't want to hurt you with this, Tammy. Believe that."

"I do. But I have to think about it."

"I understand."

She stood, lifting her purse from the chair as he walked around his desk. He drew her into his arms, wanting this to be the beginning and not an ending. He'd had enough of endings. But he couldn't think about Rachel now. Not yet.

"I'll talk to you later," she said, pulling free.

"Thank you."

"Don't thank me yet. It's not a done deal."

"I know."

She walked to the door, looked back at him once, then she was gone.

Guy sat back down at his desk, glad she'd closed the door behind her. The enormity of what he'd done had hit him hard ever since he'd woken this morning. Rachel had been snuggled up against him, warm and so beautiful in sleep it nearly killed him. He'd gotten up as quietly as possible and slipped out of her bedroom to dress. She didn't come out by the time he was finished, and he left without bothering her. He hadn't seen her today, although he knew she was here.

His disappointment at her decision was still as sharp as the moment she'd spoken the words. Now he was sorry he'd said he wouldn't press, because all he wanted to do was convince her to give them a chance. He could see so clearly how good they could be together. But that wasn't the point. *She* had to see it. What troubled him was that in a month, he wouldn't be around. She'd have plenty of time to forget him. To pretend that what they'd discovered together wasn't real.

There wasn't a damn thing he could do about it, though. Not today. Maybe he'd see a way tomorrow. All he could do was trust that in the end, the right thing would happen.

He'd told her last night that he was in love with her, and it was the truth. He was. And he wanted to spend the rest of his life discovering every nuance of who she was. What he knew for sure was that he wouldn't give up.

"IT'S ME."

"I was hoping you'd call. It's been two weeks."

"I know. I've wanted to, but I've been…busy."

"Busy."

"And crazy."

"Oh."

Rachel sat back on her bed and adjusted her covers. It was just past nine-thirty, and though she'd tried to sleep after a hellish day in the E.R., her thoughts had kept her tossing and turning, just like last night and the night before.

She heard Allie sigh on the other end of the line. "So what's up? Is this about him?"

"Yeah."

"Well, are you going to make me guess?"

"He quit."

"Oh?"

"The E.R. He quit and he's leaving in two weeks. He's keeping the baby. Heath. You know, Heather's son. His ex-wife didn't take him back to France, and Guy is going to adopt him. He's staying home to raise him."

"Wow."

"No kidding. I still hardly believe it myself. He's such a good doctor."

"Raising a child won't take away his skills."

"I know."

"And for him, maybe taking Heath is more important."

"I know that's true. I think he's made the right choice. For himself. It's just…"

"What?"

"It's huge."

"Oh, yeah. But doesn't it clear up one problem?"

"You mean that he's not my boss anymore?"

"Yep."

"It should have." Rachel got her cup of tea from the bedside table. It was hot and she blew on it before she took a sip. "It should have," she repeated, "but it didn't. After he told me, I kind of freaked. It was the whole relationship thing that scared me. Especially now that he's a single father. I mean, to take on him and his son?"

"Yeah, I can see where that would be scary."

"That's what I'm saying."

"But, Rachel?"

"Yeah."

"It's pretty obvious you aren't indifferent to the man. I can hear it in your voice. You sound horrible."

"I am."

"So what do you want?"

"To go back to the way it was."

"Too bad. So what else do you want?"

Rachel sighed. "I don't know."

"I do. You want this man. You want him in your life."

"But—"

"But nothing. It's gonna be a challenge, but so what? All relationships are a challenge. What does he want?"

"He says he loves me."

"Oh."

"Uh-huh."

"Do you love him back?"

She closed her eyes. This was the one question she wasn't willing to look at. But she supposed there was no choice. "I'm not sure."

"It's a possibility?"

"It's too soon for me to just say I love him. But I'm so miserable without him. I mean, if we hadn't… If I didn't…"

"But you did, and now—"

"Now I miss it…him."

"You know what's next, right?"

"I'm scared."

"I know."

Rachel blew out a big breath of air. "Okay. I'll seriously think about it."

"Think about it, my butt. Do something, Rachel. This is your chance, girl. Don't let it pass you by or you'll regret it the rest of your life."

"I just want to feel calm again."

"You will, as long as you walk through it. If you don't, the only thing you'll feel is dead inside."

Rachel sipped her tea again, blinking back her too familiar tears. "Okay. I'll let you know what happens."

"You'd better. I love you, you know."

"I love you, too."

"See? You're already a whiz at this love stuff. Now just spread it around."

"Good night, Allie."

"'Night."

RACHEL RANG THE BELL, then looked at the bottle in her hand. It wasn't wine this time, but champagne. The good stuff—Dom Pérignon. There was a lot to celebrate tonight, and she wanted everything to be just right. Of course he wasn't expecting her, and that could end up badly, but with what she had to tell him, the odds were in her favor.

The door opened with a rush, and the surprise on Guy's face was only surpassed by his incredible smile. "Hey."

"Hey, yourself."

"What? Why?"

"If you let me in, I'll tell you."

"Oh, sure…sure. Come in. You'll have to excuse the mess. They still haven't finished the wall in Heath's room, and there's dust everywhere."

She walked past him into the hallway, liking the hint of sawdust in the air.

"What's that?"

She held up the bottle, complete with red bow. "I come bearing gifts. And news."

"Oh?"

"But first, let me tell you again how incredibly happy I am for you. About Heath."

He walked her into the living room, his hand on the small of her back. The light touch made her quiver, and she remembered, as she had every day and night for two weeks, how he could turn her to mush. "Tammy's been great about it. I think she's satisfied that this isn't a whim. That Heath and I are together for the long haul."

"He's looking wonderful."

"I know. He'll be here next week, which is just amazing. When did you see him?"

Rachel sat on the end of the couch, and Guy sat next to her, close enough that their knees brushed. "This afternoon. He's really grown. And he's so beautiful. Just like his mother."

Guy smiled with pride. "I've started the adoption procedures."

She grinned. "Talk about your perfect segues."

"And that means…?"

"I got a phone call about an hour ago. From a friend of yours."

"Oh?"

"Richie Montgomery."

"You're kidding."

"Nope."

He scooted closer. "Come on, don't kill me here."

"Okay, okay. They found him."

"Oh, God."

She gripped his hand. "He's in jail, Guy. DiGrasso was caught selling drugs in Van Nuys. A lot of them. It's going to be decades before he's on the street again. But that's not all."

"I don't know if I can take more."

"Oh," she said, sitting back. "Okay."

"Damn it, woman, speak!"

She laughed. "Stan told them everything about the adoption agency people. What they did, how they ran the operation, and the best part is, he told the police where to find them. They might be in custody even now."

Guy stood up and pulled her into his arms. He hugged her until it hurt, but she didn't care. This was the best news in the world, and she was incredibly grateful that Richie had called her first.

She sniffed, her tears wetting Guy's T-shirt, but she didn't care. What had started with such tragedy was ending with something she couldn't have imagined. Hope. Stan was off the street, those agency bastards would never destroy another life, and Heath had the best father in the world.

"Oh, baby, I can't believe this. Thank you, thank you."

"I didn't do a thing," Rachel protested.

He pulled back so he could look at her. "Are you kidding?"

"I didn't," she said. She could feel her heart speed up, and she had to swallow before she could go on. "But I want to."

Guy's thick eyebrows nearly met as he frowned in confusion. "What?"

"Callie Baker offered me the job."

Rachel could see he was struggling to be happy for her. To celebrate. But he couldn't quite do it, and she didn't want to make him suffer.

"I turned it down," she said.

"Why?"

"Because I don't want to spend more hours at the hospital."

He stepped back a little, but his hands were still on her arms. "No?"

She shook her head. "I want time to spend with you."

He swallowed, his Adam's apple rising and falling, but he didn't say a word. She didn't think he could.

"I've done a lot of thinking, and I can't make any promises, but I miss you. A whole lot more than I thought I would."

"I know just how that feels."

"It's awful. I can't tell you that it's going to be all hearts and flowers, but I'd like to give it a shot."

"Even with Heath?"

"Oh, yeah."

Guy took in a huge breath of air and let it out really slowly. Then his grip on her arms tightened and he pulled her close. Close enough to kiss.

Rachel melted into his arms, so incredibly glad to be back there. She parted her lips, and he slipped inside, and it was the most wonderful moment… The start of a whole new life. A whole new way of seeing the world.

And the best part was, they were going to do it together.

*Ordinary people. Extraordinary circumstances.
Meet a new generation of heroes—
the men and women of
Courage Bay Emergency Services.*
CODE RED
*A new Harlequin continuity series continues
February 2005 with*

*TREMORS
By Debra Webb*

*An earthquake collapses a parking garage. A woman
is trapped, a support pillar pressing down on her
SUV. Fire Captain Joe Ripani won't risk his men—the
rescue is too dangerous. He'll go in alone....
Here's a preview!*

She was dreaming of him again.

She knew better…but she dreamed anyway.

Dreamed of making slow, sweet love.

Dreamed of all the fantasies that he'd instilled deep within her heart during their short time together.

Dreamed of picket fences and the pitter-patter of little feet.

Lisa Malloy stirred…the hard facts of reality prodding her from the dreams she so wanted to believe could come true.

But Joe Ripani wasn't a forever kind of guy. He wasn't even a real relationship guy.

Lisa moaned softly and tried to surface from what had turned quickly into an unpleasant nightmare.

She wanted to cling to the hope that Joe would somehow morph into the kind of man she longed to spend forever with, but deep inside she knew the truth. Their short affair—had been all they would ever have. End of subject.

Her head hurt.

Or maybe it was her heart…or both.

She had to wake up. There was a very good reason she shouldn't be sleeping right now.

Something was very, very wrong.

Wake up.

Another groan seeped past her lips. Why couldn't she wake up? Why did her head hurt so badly?

Wake up!

She had to take the first step…had to open her eyes.

"Mmm," she murmured softly. God, what was that pounding in her skull?

Lisa's eyes fluttered open.

She never took afternoon naps.

What was wrong with her?

Surely this wasn't another symptom of…

Her gaze focused on something in front of her, drawing her full attention in that direction.

Steering wheel.

Windshield.

Cracked glass.

What the…?

The memory of her SUV shuddering beneath her…the odd up and down motion that felt as if she'd been driving over a bumpy road when she hadn't even started the engine…zoomed into her head with a sensory detonation that made her groan even louder. She'd gotten into the vehicle after her visit to her tax accountant's office. She remembered closing the door. And then the sudden vibrations…

The distinct whine of metal made her breath catch.

Lisa's gaze jerked upward.

It took a full five seconds for her brain to absorb and comprehend what her eyes saw.

The roof of her SUV was dented…jutting downward…only inches from her head.

How was that possible?

Her vision blurred and she squeezed her eyes shut to slow the spinning inside her head.

Pull it together, she ordered her mind, which instantly tried to go fuzzy on her again.

Had she been in an accident?

Earthquake. The word surfaced through her confusion, and she knew without further examination that one had occurred. That's why she'd felt the vehicle moving even before she started the engine.

But she was safe…inside the parking garage.

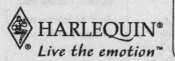

SAGA

USA TODAY bestselling author

JOAN ELLIOTT PICKART

brings you a brand-new story in her bestselling MacAllister family saga...

MacAllister's
Return

When Assistant D.A. Jesse Burke
finds out that he was stolen as a
baby, he heads to California to
discover his true heritage—and
finds unexpected love with
TV news anchor Krista Kelly.

**"Joan Elliott Pickart gives a delightful read via
inviting characters and a soft and light style."**
—*Romantic Times*

Coming in January 2005.

Where love comes alive™

**Exclusive
Bonus Features:**

**Author Interview
Sneak Preview...
and more!**

SPOTLIGHT

"Debra Webb's fast-paced thriller will make you shiver in passion and fear...."—*Romantic Times*

Dying To Play

Debra Webb

When FBI agent Trace Callahan arrives in Atlanta to investigate a baffling series of multiple homicides, deputy chief of detectives Elaine Jentzen isn't prepared for the immediate attraction between them. And as they hunt to find the killer known as the Gamekeeper, it seems that Trace is singled out as his next victim...unless Elaine can stop the Gamekeeper before it's too late.

Available January 2005.

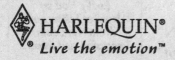
Live the emotion™

> **Exclusive Bonus Features:**
> Author Interview
> Sneak Preview...
> and more!